DOG IN THE DUGOUT

JODY STUDDARD

Dog in the Dugout

This is a work of fiction.
The characters, names, incidents,
and dialogue are products
of the author's imagination.

Cover Design: Jody Studdard

ISBN-13: 978-1489583376
ISBN-10: 1489583378

For Debbie and Shelby

August 25

Today was the best day of my life. I've wanted a puppy for as long as I can remember and, after years of groveling, my dad finally agreed I could get one, but only on one condition. I had to hit a home run in today's game against the Edmonds Express.

I was excited but I knew it wasn't going to be easy. The Express' pitcher, Amy Adams, was really good, and when I say really good, I mean really, really, really good. She threw super hard and had a bunch of different pitches, including a nasty changeup that was nearly impossible to hit. I've never seen a girl throw a changeup as well as her. It was at least fifteen miles per hour slower than her other pitches and she used it to strike me out during my first two at-bats.

But that wasn't my biggest concern. My biggest concern was I had never hit a home run before. Never. In my entire life. I've played fastpitch softball for as long as I can remember and I'm a good hitter most days, but for some strange reason I had never hit a home run.

But then again, I had never had so much at stake. I wanted that puppy and I wanted it bad. So I was going to hit a home run if it killed me.

I took a deep breath as I stepped into the batter's box. I dug my cleats into the dirt. I was nervous. Big time. It was the bottom of the seventh inning so it was my final chance. I glanced at the stands and saw my dad sitting in the bleachers with the rest of the parents, watching attentively, like he did at all of my games. My team, the Seattle Sky, was losing 6-5 with two outs, but the bases were loaded so everyone was hoping I'd get a hit and we'd come from behind to win.

But I didn't care about that.

All I cared about was that puppy.

The first pitch was a fastball, high and away. I knew I shouldn't swing at it because it wasn't a strike, but I was too excited and I swung anyway.

"Strike one," blue shouted. In softball, we call the umpires blue because they usually wear blue uniforms.

I glanced at the stands. The parents, and especially my dad, weren't happy with that swing at all.

The next pitch was in the dirt, for a ball, as was the one after that, but the fourth was pure heat. It went by me so fast I didn't even have a chance to swing at it.

Blue's response was immediate. "Strike two."

I called for time and stepped out of the batter's box. My coach, John Smith, sent me signals from his position in the third base coach's box, but I wasn't paying attention, not at all. I was down to my last chance. One more strike and it was over. If I missed the next pitch, I could kiss that puppy goodbye.

Luckily for me, I didn't miss the next pitch. Amy tried to finish me off with her patented changeup, just like she had done earlier in the game, but I was ready this time. I kept my hands back until the very last second, then swung with everything I had. My bat was nothing but a blur as it made contact with its target.

And I didn't just hit it. I crushed it. The Express' outfielders didn't even try to catch it; they just turned and watched as it soared into the distance. It cleared the outfield fence by at least twenty feet, probably more.

When I got to home plate, my teammates tackled me. It was a classic pig pile and I had tears of joy in my eyes. Everyone thought I was happy because I had just won the game, but my happiness had nothing to do with that. All I cared about was my puppy. I could hardly believe it but I had done it.

And believe it or not, I had already picked out a name for the little guy.

Homer.

August 26

Homer is the greatest puppy ever. I got him from a friend of mine, Lea Levin. Lea is one of my teammates on the Sky, our first baseman, and her dog, Molly, just had a litter of puppies. My dad and I drove to her house in Marysville, which is about twenty miles north of my house in Seattle. When we got there, all of the puppies were in a makeshift pen Lea's dad had constructed in the garage. They were so cute. They were half chocolate Labrador and half Chow, so they pretty much looked like chocolate Labradors but they had black tongues like Chows. And they had big, floppy ears. There were ten of them but two had already been claimed by other people so there were eight left for me to pick from. I took turns holding at least five of them, but they all seemed so gorgeous I couldn't decide which one to get. One of them licked me on the face, which was slimy but I liked it anyway, one of them tried to play tug-of-war with the collar on my coat, and another squiggled out of my arms and raced off across the floor. It took Lea and I five minutes to catch him.

Luckily, my dad solved the problem for me. He took an old, weathered softball from a shelf on a nearby wall and tossed it into the pen. All of the puppies ignored it except one. He was sleeping on the far side of the cage, on a little pile of rags, completely by himself. To be honest, I had been so distracted by the other puppies I hadn't even noticed him. He was by far the smallest of the group and was definitely the runt of the litter, but he was absolutely adorable, with big ears and the brightest eyes I had ever seen. He jumped up as soon as the softball rolled past him and chased after it. He tried to get it in his mouth and pick it up, but it was too big for him, and all he managed to do was lose his balance, fall over the top of it, and flip completely onto his back. But he wasn't discouraged, not in the least, not for a second. He scrambled to his feet and darted after it again, trying to get control of it once more. It looked like a wrestling match between a puppy and a softball and somehow the softball was winning.

My decision was made. "That's him. That's Homer."

Ten minutes later, we were back in the car heading for home and I was the happiest girl on the planet.

August 27

Life is good when you have a puppy. Today Homer followed me everywhere, except when he got tired and needed a nap, which happened about once every twenty minutes. Everything he did was so cute. He couldn't get into our living room because it's sunken and he's too small to get down the step leading into it from the hallway. So I teased him by going into it without him and he howled in agony every time I did it. In the future, I probably shouldn't do that too much more or I might give him a bad case of separation anxiety.

He's completely loaded with toys. My dad and I went to the pet store and spoiled him rotten. He's got all kinds of stuffed animals, squeaky toys, and rawhide bones, and one of the rawhide bones is so big he can't even lift it, but he likes it anyway. My dad thought it was hilarious to watch him try to carry a bone around the kitchen that was almost as big as he was, and I must admit it was indeed pretty funny, especially when he tried to pick it up and ended up flipping completely onto his back in the process.

But my cat wasn't happy at all. His name was Cinnamon and I'd had him since I was eight, so he was seven. He was big and orange, with a plump belly and a long tail that was striped like a raccoon. He was my only pet until then so he was used to having my complete and undivided attention. He wasn't happy about having a dog in the house, not in the least. He gave Homer a nasty look, and when Homer ran over to say hi to him, Cinnamon slapped him on the nose. And he slapped him hard. Homer yelped and jumped back so quickly he hit one of my mom's decorative plastic plants and knocked it into the fireplace. Luckily my dad got to it quickly and saved it from catching on fire. In the meantime, I rescued Homer. He wasn't hurt badly but he did have a speck of blood on his nose where he had been slapped.

That reminded me. I needed to clip Cinnamon's claws.

Unfortunately, Homer hadn't learned his lesson. He wanted so badly to be friends with Cinnamon he wandered over to him again, about a half hour later, this time a little more cautiously than before, and he tried to give him a sniff. Unfortunately, the result was the same as the first time. Cinnamon reached out with one paw, claws out, ready to strike. But this time I was ready and I jumped in the middle to protect Homer from the ensuing blow.

But then I realized something. I was the one who was going to get the slap.

And he slapped me good. Right in the side of the leg, just above my calf, with full claws out. It left a nasty scratch, at least an inch long, and it hurt like a beast. I was so angry I grabbed Cinnamon and headed for our sliding glass door, which leads out to the back yard. "You're gonna spend the night outside, bad cat. And don't come back until you've worked on that attitude a little."

I tossed him onto the porch and returned to Homer. He wagged his tail and looked up at me with his big, droopy, brown eyes.

"Don't worry," I told him. "You have nothing to worry about. That mean cat won't hurt you any more."

August 28

Homer loves to play fetch. I didn't even have to teach him. Somehow, inherently, he just knew how. We couldn't use a softball since a softball is too big for his mouth, but he had no problem with a tennis ball. We played for about ten minutes and everything was great fun until I tossed the ball into the hallway and it went down the staircase. Homer raced after it as fast as he could but he didn't realize how slick the hardwood floor was, slipped on it, and fell down the staircase.

I nearly freaked out as I watched him bounce head-over-paws down the steps. But amazingly, once he got to the bottom, he popped up and headed after the ball, completely unfazed, like nothing unusual or dangerous had even happened. After retrieving the ball, however, he turned and realized something. He was too small to make it back up the stairs to me at the top. No matter how hard he tried, he just couldn't get his tummy up and over the steps. After five minutes of frantic struggling, he somehow had made it to the third step, but then he lost his balance and tumbled all of the way to the bottom again. So finally he gave up, sat down, and shot me an irresistible 'please help the puppy' look that I couldn't resist. I ran down the stairs and carried him back to the top.

Not too long after that, I gave him his first bath. I don't think he really needed it because he was already pretty clean, but what the heck. The day before, my dad and I had gotten some shampoo and a brush when we were at the pet store and I wanted to see how well they worked. My older sister, Chloe, joined in and helped me wash him. He was so small he fit in the kitchen sink with ease and he loved the attention, especially when Chloe and I started scrubbing him at the same time. My mom wasn't too enthusiastic about us giving a dog a bath in "her kitchen" but she got over it quickly. Which was good, because my dog was going to get pampered whether she liked it or not.

My dad and I set up a kennel for Homer downstairs in the family room and I decided to stay with him for the night. My room is upstairs, with the other bedrooms, but I didn't want to leave him alone since he's still getting acclimated to our house and still getting used to being away from his mother and siblings. I was afraid he'd get lonely if I left him by himself for too long. I put him in his kennel and closed the gate, but he didn't like that at all and banged on the gate repeatedly with one paw, so I let him out and he slept with me in a sleeping bag on the couch.

It doesn't get much better than that. A girl and her dog. It's a match made in heaven. I should have hit that home run years ago.

August 29

It isn't easy owning a puppy. This morning, Homer had an accident on the living room carpet.

And on the family room carpet.

And on the dining room carpet.

And on the bedroom carpet.

I didn't understand what the problem was. I took him outside every twenty minutes to take care of business, but whenever we went outside, he never had to go. He'd just spend his time sniffing around the yard and he'd chase after butterflies whenever he spotted one. He really liked the bright yellow ones that have black dots. As soon as I brought him back inside the house, there was an accident.

My mom was furious. Apparently, the carpet was precious to her. She got our steam cleaner out of the hallway closet and made me clean the floor meticulously after each accident. Homer didn't like the steam cleaner at all. It was so loud it scared him, so he ran down the hall and hid in the dining room under the table until I was done.

That wasn't the only problem. He wouldn't sleep, either. At least not by himself. The night before, I didn't mind sleeping with him downstairs in the family room on the couch, but tonight I was pretty tired so I wanted to sleep in my room in my bed. As you can probably imagine, my bed is a lot more comfortable than the couch in the family room. But Homer would have none of it. As soon as I put him in his kennel, turned out the light, and left the room, he started barking.

My dad had a suggestion. "Don't worry about it. Just ignore him and he'll stop barking in a couple of minutes."

He didn't. It went on for an hour straight, with him barking as loud as he could the whole time. Finally, my dad got mad and shouted at me, "Get down there and do something about that dog."

So I went downstairs, got him, brought him up to my room, and let him sleep with me in my bed. That worked great, at least at first, and he slept perfectly until 3:30 in the morning. Then, much to my chagrin, he was wide awake and ready to frolic. So I put him on the floor, hoping he would keep himself busy with his chew toys and I could resume some much-needed shut-eye, but then he had an accident on the carpet. So I scooped him up and took him outside. And then I stood with him outside, in the cold, for twenty minutes as he did absolutely nothing except chase after a hummingbird.

Ugh.

September 7

It's getting old fast. It's been almost two weeks now and no matter what I do, no matter what I try, Homer will not stay in his kennel downstairs, and he will never sleep all night. So I'm getting pretty tired. It's not easy getting up every day at 3:30 in the morning.

And it's ruined my social life. Not to say I ever had much of a social life, but now I never get to do anything. I mean, I can't leave Homer alone by himself, he's just too small. Maybe when he gets a little older, but for now . . .

The final insult happened this evening. Cinnamon sat on the back of the living room couch, watching me, as I cleaned up another of Homer's accidents. Cinnamon has always been an arrogant cat, ever since he was a kitten, and he gave me one of those smug 'I told you so' looks. He thought he was so smart.

Stupid cat. I should have gotten rid of him years ago. But then again, at least he's disciplined and doesn't have accidents on the carpet.

September 8

My dad and I took Homer to a dog park for the first time today. It was pretty fun but Homer surprised me. He didn't like the other dogs, not at all. He bumped noses and sniffed them a little, but other than that he didn't want anything to do with them. But he loved all of the people who were there and he made friends with everyone. They all thought he was adorable and they were amazed how soft his fur was. A lady with red hair asked if I gave him a bath every day, and I responded that I didn't, and it had actually been several days since his last bath. His hair is naturally soft and shiny. I wish I could say the same thing about mine, especially today. Despite my best efforts and at least thirty minutes in the bathroom, it looked like a complete mess.

Anyway, the dog park is located on a long, rocky beach on the east side of Puget Sound, so my dad got this brilliant idea to put Homer in the water.

"He's part Labrador. He'll love the water. Labradors always do. They're strong swimmers."

Homer hated it. The minute my dad placed him in the water, a wave came in and washed right over him, soaking him to the bone. He climbed to shore and looked like a shivering, wet, mangy mess. He even had a strand of seaweed on one side of his head.

"Good idea, dad." There was more than a little sarcasm in my voice. I got a blanket from our car, wrapped it around Homer, and dried him off. He was freezing.

My dad shrugged. "Maybe he'll like it when he's older."

After the dog park, we took him to a pet store but that didn't go over too well because a mean poodle bullied him. I didn't know the words 'mean' and 'poodle' could be used in the same sentence but trust me, they can. That poodle was fierce. It was one of those big, mutant types that look like a normal poodle but are freakishly tall. How did that happen? Was it a genetic experiment gone wrong? Anyway, it bared its teeth and growled menacingly so Homer stayed as far away from it as he could.

But then we found something he really liked. And when I say really, I mean really with a capital R.

Softball practice.

At least once a week, my dad, Chloe, and I practice at McCall Park, which is a group of Little League softball fields not too far from our house. It's actually within walking distance but we were too lazy to walk, so we drove instead, and we took Homer with us. He sat on one side of the field, near first base, and watched attentively as my dad pitched a bucket of Wiffle balls to Chloe and me. Wiffle balls are small, about the size of a golf ball, made of white plastic, and hollow, and we use a stick bat to hit them. A stick bat is a small, thin bat used by players during practice drills and training exercises. Since it is thinner than a normal bat it makes it a lot harder to hit the balls, so you really have to work on your focus and hand-eye coordination. We finished a bucket of balls and I put my stick bat down near home plate so I could help my dad and Chloe round everything up for another round, but when I came back to get it, it was gone. I looked all over and finally spotted Homer, who was now standing at third base, with it in his mouth.

"Silly dog. Give that back."

I walked up to him and tried to take it from him, but he darted away just as I got within arm's reach. I raced after him, and he ran away again, and after that the chase was officially on. He darted to second base, then to first, then to home, and then back to third. I raced after him but darn, for a puppy, he's fast. I finally caught up to him and got my bat back, but when I looked up I saw my dad standing there with a stopwatch in his hand.

"I should have thought of that years ago. That's the fastest I've seen you run in years, Angel. That was one of your best times ever from base-to-base."

"Very funny, dad." I wasn't amused, but I had to admit, it had been a good workout. I was covered in sweat and still breathing heavily.

And unfortunately, it wasn't my last workout for the day. After we completed the next bucket of balls, I set my stick bat back down on the ground and guess who grabbed it and ran off?

That darn dog.

September 10

Something interesting happened at school today. I met a boy. Well, I didn't actually meet him, but I saw him. I was sitting in the school's cafeteria, eating lunch with my friends, Lea Levin (I got Homer from her) and Kimi Sasaki, and like always Kimi was complaining about her mom who owns a teriyaki restaurant and makes Kimi work at it after school, when a boy walked by I had never seen before. He wasn't too tall and was actually a little on the stocky side, but he had wide, muscular shoulders, thick arms, and short, shaggy, blond hair. His eyes were blue and sparkled in the light. He carried a tray of food and sat down with some of the school's football players at a table in the middle of the room.

My school, Monroe High, is a big place and being a freshman I was new there, so there were a lot of people I didn't know, but there was something about this boy that caught my attention and really made him stand out.

"Who's that?"

Lea's answer was immediate. "Logan McCoy. He's a new kid, a sophomore. He transferred here from some school in Texas. Something happened with his family so he's living with his uncle for a year."

"What happened?"

"I'm not certain. But he's supposed to be really nice and they say he's an incredible football player. He was the starting halfback on his team in Texas last year even though he was just a freshman. Word is he's probably going to be our starter this year."

Kimi raised an eyebrow. "I thought Travis Henry was our starter."

"He was. But apparently Logan is better. And he's dreamy. Just look at him."

Lea didn't need to tell me; I already was. To be honest, I was staring at him. There was something about him that mesmerized me. I didn't know if it was because he was new to our school, or because he was from somewhere so far away, or maybe it was because he was so attractive, but regardless, I couldn't focus on anything else the rest of the day. No matter how hard I tried, I kept thinking about him.

Which was really bad, since I had a pop quiz in my math class. I haven't gotten the results back yet and I don't want to. It's not going to be pretty.

September 11

I need a bigger bed. Mine is too small because Homer and Cinnamon sleep with me every night. Cinnamon sleeps on one side, Homer sleeps on the other, and I'm squeezed in between like a sardine. And Cinnamon takes up a lot of room because he doesn't sleep like a normal cat and instead sleeps on his back with his legs stretched out as far as they will go. And Homer isn't much better, because he's grown a lot since I first got him and he now takes up nearly as much room as Cinnamon.

Both animals are ridiculous at times. They are super competitive with one another and get jealous whenever I give too much attention to the other. Usually, Homer doesn't bark too much, but he gets anxious and barks at Cinnamon if I pet him for too long. And Cinnamon doesn't like to be barked at, so he gets mad and hisses at Homer. But both seem to be tolerating each other now, which is good. Homer still wants to be friends with Cinnamon and Cinnamon seems to be getting used to having Homer around, but he's still not too happy about it and there is an occasional smack on the nose.

September 12

Homer learned a new trick today. My dad, Chloe, and I went to McCall Park to practice, and, like the first time we took him, he sat patiently on one side of the field as my dad pitched a bucket of Wiffle balls to us. But about halfway through the bucket, he trotted onto the field, picked up one of the Wiffle balls in his mouth, carried it over to the bucket, and dropped it inside.

There was an amazed look on my dad's face. "Did you see that? Did you teach him that?"

I shook my head. I was as amazed as he was.

"Do it again, Homer."

So he did. He trotted over to another ball, one I had hit down the first base foul line, grabbed it, brought it back, and plopped it into the bucket.

"That's awesome," Chloe said.

Practice went on from there and it was great. With Homer picking up the balls for us, as Chloe and I hit them, it sped things up and made it a much more productive workout. Normally during a practice, we do ten buckets total and it takes us about half an hour. But today, with Homer's help, it only took fifteen minutes. So that freed up more time to work on other things like throwing and fielding.

"That's an amazing dog," my dad said as we headed for home.

Homer barked. That was his way of saying he agreed.

September 13

Today I went to the football game. I'd like to say I went because I love football and wanted to show my school spirit, but to be completely honest, I really just went to see Logan. I've been fascinated with him since I saw him that day in the cafeteria, and I've been hearing around school how good he is, so I wanted to see for myself if it was true.

I wasn't disappointed. Like always, the stadium was packed and extremely festive, with cheerleaders jumping around, the band playing music, and the team's mascot dancing on the edge of the field, but the real excitement didn't begin until the teams took the field. As predicted and despite only being a sophomore, Logan had won our team's halfback position, so he took the field with the starters. I don't know too much about football so I don't really know what was going on, but apparently things started well. Our quarterback, who is a junior named Caleb Smith, took the snap, handed the ball to Logan, and he ran through a small opening in the line of really big players up front. I forget what they're called, tightguards or linetackles or something like that, but anyway, he made his way past them, darted to the left, then ran twenty yards before the defenders caught him and dragged him down from behind. Everyone in the stands went crazy and the cheerleaders waved their pompoms in celebration. One girl did a backflip, which, to me, was almost as impressive as Logan's run. The next play was more of the same. Caleb took the snap, dropped back to make a pass but couldn't find any receivers to throw the ball to, so he turned and tossed it to Logan, who had had left his starting position and drifted to the right near the far sideline. Logan caught the ball in stride and darted forward, dodging two defenders before finally being forced out of bounds by a third. It wasn't quite as long a run as the first one, but it was good nonetheless. Everyone cheered and the players patted Logan on the back.

I sat there in complete awe. He wasn't good. He was spectacular. He made one great play after another. In no time, we were ahead 14-0 and he scored both of the touchdowns, one on a short run up the middle and another on a pass from Caleb into the corner of the endzone.

But the highlight of the game, by far, happened in the fourth quarter. There were only a few minutes remaining on the scoreboard and we were ahead 35-0. Logan had just scored another touchdown, and as he headed to the sideline to get a drink and take a break, he looked up into the bleachers, right where I was standing. For a brief second, our eyes met and he smiled at me and instantly I knew what needed to be done. I needed to meet him. And I needed to do it soon.

September 14

Today I found something Homer likes even more than practicing softball at McCall Park with my dad, Chloe, and me. He likes practicing with my team. I play for the Seattle Sky, a 16u select team made up of girls from all over the Seattle metropolitan area. My dad and I took Homer to practice today and the girls on the team swarmed him the minute he hopped out of the car. And of course he loved the attention and had plenty of kisses to give them in return.

Lea, who hadn't seen him since the day we got him from her house, was amazed. "He's grown so much. But he's as adorable as ever."

The other girls were in complete agreement.

"He's the cutest dog I've ever seen," Kimi said.

"I want one just like him," Haley Jones said. She's our second baseman. She's a small girl with blonde hair and long bangs. Homer gave her a really wet kiss right on the side of the face.

We led him into our dugout and he seemed right at home. He sniffed around under the bench for a couple of minutes, took a quick look at our bats hanging in the bat rack and our bags hanging on the wall, then rushed back to the girls to get some more attention. Haley took a bandana out of her softball bag and wrapped it around his neck. It had our team colors (blue and gray) and our logo (the word Sky shaped like a lightning bolt) on it.

"There. Now it's official. He's our mascot."

Even our coaches liked him. They started laughing when they sent us to do our warm-up laps and he followed us. But he didn't remain following for long. Homer loves to run and he has limitless energy, so after the first lap he darted to the front of the group and led us from there. He'd even slow up on occasion so he could look back and make certain we were all keeping up. After our warm-up laps, we did our stretching and other beginning-of-practice exercises, including pushups and crunches. The coaches laughed as Homer strolled up and down our lines and barked at any girl who wasn't doing a good job.

"He's great," Coach Smith said. "He's like a little drill sergeant."

After that, we did numerous other drills, sometimes as a large group and sometimes at different stations in groups of two or three. Homer roamed the field like he owned the place and he helped everywhere he could. When I was batting, I hit a ball and it went over the fence and into a nearby parking lot. Homer darted after it, grabbed it (he's big enough now he can pick up softballs), and brought it back.

The only bad part of practice happened a few minutes later. Our third baseman is a tall girl named Casey Morgan, and she has a really strong arm, but she has control problems on occasion.

Some of the other girls call her 'Wild Arm Morgan' behind her back. Anyway, she threw one ball too high and it flew across the field and nailed Homer right in the side. He wasn't hurt but boy did it anger Coach Smith.

"Casey! Did you hit our new mascot?"

Casey didn't know what to say so she just stood there with a stupid look on her face.

Coach Smith continued. "We have a new rule, effective immediately. Anyone who hits the team mascot owes me a lap. Get moving, Casey."

But he wasn't done. He turned to Homer and said, "You lead her. And make certain she doesn't dog it."

Everyone except Casey laughed at his pun.

Off they went. Casey did her lap around the field, and Homer led her the whole way. And normally Casey would have been mad since no one likes doing a punishment lap, but since she had Homer with her, it didn't seem too bad. And Homer wasn't mad even though Casey had hit him with the ball, because that's just how he is. He doesn't get mad and he never holds a grudge. Everything was settled for good at the end of the lap when Casey apologized to Homer and gave him a big kiss on top of the head.

September 16

This weekend, my team had a tournament in Tacoma, a city about thirty miles south of Seattle. Our first game was against a team called the LadyCats. We were really excited because this was our first game with an 'official' mascot. Homer sat in our dugout and watched attentively, with his team bandana wrapped proudly around his neck. His eyes were bright and I could tell he was loving every minute of it.

During my first at-bat, I fouled a pitch away and the ball cleared the fence and went into a flower bed. Homer darted from his spot in the dugout, grabbed it, and ran back toward the field.

Blue saw what he had done and turned to me with a puzzled look on his face. "What's he doing?"

My answer was matter-of-fact. "He's getting the ball for you. He likes to help."

Homer ran up to Blue and dropped the ball at his feet.

Blue looked amazed. "I'll be darned. I should have thought of this years ago. Thank you, fella."

"His name's Homer."

"Thank you, Homer." Blue reached down and patted Homer on the head.

Homer returned to our dugout and the game continued from there, with Homer retrieving foul balls whenever we hit them. And Blue loved it, because it sped up the game and made things a lot easier for him. Normally, he had to find someone to go and get the ball for him and sometimes there were delays as a result. With Homer involved, delays were a thing of the past.

If that wasn't good enough, it was a great game. The LadyCats are a really good team, with solid players at every position, and they led for most of the way but we came back and won it in the final inning when Casey hit a double off of the outfield wall that scored Lea all of the way from first. Lea is really fast and she slid under the catcher's tag with ease. I played the whole game in my normal position at short and I got two hits, a double in the second inning and a triple in the fifth. The triple got me two RBIs.

Our second game was almost as noteworthy. It was against a team from Wenatchee called the Wings, and it went well until the fifth inning. Our starting pitcher is a girl named Laura King and our backup is her identical twin sister Hannah. They both play catcher, too, so when one girl is pitching, the other catches. Laura started to struggle and she gave up two hits in a row so Coach Smith decided to take her out and replace her with Hannah. Unfortunately, Laura didn't want to stop pitching since she thought she was doing fine, and Hannah didn't want to take over since she didn't feel like pitching. So the girls did what they always did when presented with that situation. They went into the dugout, waited until Coach Smith wasn't watching, and switched jerseys. They had been doing this for years and all of the other girls knew about it, but remarkably Coach Smith had never figured it out. He cheered as Laura walked back onto the field and, now pitching as Hannah, struck out the next batter with ease.

"That's why I made the change. Laura did a great job today but she was clearly out of gas. Everyone could see it. I doubt she would have lasted another batter or two."

He never knew it, but she did. She pitched the rest of the game and she didn't give up another hit the entire way, and we ended up winning 7-6. I got two doubles and a sacrifice, and I stole two bases, which is one of my favorite things in the entire world. There's nothing quite like the flood of adrenaline you get when you take off and you know it's you versus the catcher. It's a complete thrill every time. Unless you get out, of course.

But our third game was a disappointment. It got cancelled. Looking back, I guess I should have seen it coming. It had been getting cloudier and cloudier as the day progressed so I guess it was just a matter of time before the raindrops began. I don't know why they call Washington the Evergreen state. I guess it's because of all of the evergreen trees that grow here, and they are pretty trees, but to be honest if I were queen for a day, I'd rename it the Evergray state. Everything in Washington is gray. The buildings are gray, the streets are gray, even the sky is gray, most of the time. And even my team is gray. We're called the Seattle Sky but we wear gray uniforms. If that doesn't tell you something, I don't know what does.

September 18

You won't hear me say this very often, but today was a great day at school. I was standing at my locker with Lea, discussing our geography homework assignment, when I spotted Logan at his locker down the hall. He was at the far end of the building and there were a lot of kids in between us but apparently my vision is pretty good because I could see him as clear as day. Like always, he looked great and he was wearing a Seahawks jersey, one of the bright green ones with the number twelve, and that immediately caught my attention. Since he was from Texas, it was unlikely he was a Seahawks fan, but it was probably his way of trying to fit in with the rest of us a little better. Anyway, he placed two books in his locker, pulled a notebook out, then turned to the left and looked right at me. Just like at the football game, my heart raced the second he did it.

Normally, I don't like to be too open with my emotions but I couldn't help it. "I want to meet him so bad."

Lea chuckled. "Doesn't everybody? He's dreamy. Why don't you go over and say hi? It can't do any harm."

I was aghast. "Just walk up to him? I don't know about that. I'm not usually that outright, especially with boys."

"Just use the old book drop trick. It works every time."

I raised an eyebrow. "Book drop? What do you mean?"

"Just walk past him and accidentally drop your books at his feet." She used her fingers to put air quotes around the word 'accidentally.' "He'll help you pick them up and hopefully say something and things will flow from there."

I was pretty skeptical. And when I say 'pretty' I mean 'completely.'

"I don't know. That sounds pretty corny to me."

"Trust me. It works every time. That's how I hooked up with Tom Ottweiler."

I couldn't believe what I had just heard. "Tom Ottweiler was a jerk. You broke up with him less than a week after you met him."

Lea shrugged. "True. But at least I got to meet him and find out for myself. How are you going to find out anything about Logan if you just stand over here on the opposite end of the hallway staring at him all day? Go over there and give it a try. You'll thank me later."

"What if it doesn't work? What if he doesn't like me? I'll be depressed for a month, probably longer."

She shrugged. "If it doesn't work, I'll take you to Starbucks and buy you a salted caramel mocha with extra whipped cream. If that doesn't make you feel better nothing will."

I smiled and I have to admit it was a pretty good response. I loved salted caramel mochas, especially with whipped cream.

I still had serious misgivings about Lea's book drop plan, but she had a point. If I ever wanted to meet Logan, and I definitely did, I needed to take the initiative and do something. Standing around gawking at him was going to accomplish nothing. As such, I grabbed a stack of books from my locker, arranged them just right so I could drop them without damaging them too badly, if at all, and headed in his direction. But I was really nervous and I started to have second thoughts the minute I got near him, and, not even realizing what I was doing, I just stopped and stood there, frozen in place for several really long seconds. And while I stood there, trying to decide if I was actually going to go through with it or not, the most amazing thing happened. Another girl, a sophomore in my math class named Hailey Wetmore, stepped in front of me, walked up to Logan, and dropped her books at his feet.

A surprised look crossed her face. "Oh my goodness. How clumsy of me."

Reflexively, Logan bent down and helped her pick up her books.

I stood there in complete shock. I couldn't believe what had happened. Hailey had beaten me to the punch. And she had used the exact same book drop plan I had been planning to use. If I had had a gun, I would have shot myself right there on the spot.

It was at that point I heard Logan's voice for the first time. It wasn't as thick as some southern accents I've heard, but it was unmistakable nonetheless. And it was exotic and intoxicating, at least to me. "Let me help you with that." He grabbed Hailey's books off of the floor, organized them neatly into a stack for her, and handed them back.

"You're so kind, Logan." She fluttered her eyelashes at him. Up until then, I had never noticed how long Hailey's eyelashes were. I had to give her credit. They were undoubtedly the longest and nicest eyelashes I had ever seen. "It's Logan, right?"

He nodded. "You're Bailey, right? You're one of the cheerleaders?"

She smiled, somewhat awkwardly. "Actually, it's Hailey. With an H."

Logan was immediately apologetic. "Sorry. I've never been good with names. Anyway, I saw you at the game Friday night. I saw you do a back flip. You were awesome."

Her eyes got big. "Thanks. It took me quite a while to master that flip."

"I wish I could do that. It would be a great celebration, especially if I did it in the endzone after scoring a touchdown."

She smiled at him, but then there was a long, awkward silence as they both stood there, looking at one another, not saying a thing. Clearly, neither of them knew what to do next. I didn't know what to do, either. I just stood there, less than five feet away, staring right at them.

Finally, Hailey broke the silence.

"So anyway, Logan, I was wondering, since you're new in town and it doesn't seem like you have a girlfriend or anything, maybe you'd like to grab some dinner. Maybe tonight if you're free."

Logan wasted no time with his response. "I'm flattered, Bailey, I truly am. But unfortunately, tonight isn't good for me. I have practice after school and then I promised my uncle I'd help him with some things around the house. Chores and stuff. It's kinda silly but you know how it is with family."

A look of complete disbelief formed on Hailey's face. Like most cheerleaders, she was mega-hot, with long legs and a big chest, so she wasn't used to being turned down. To be honest, it had probably never happened before. She was speechless and she had no idea what to do next. After a couple of long, tense, extremely uncomfortable seconds, and without saying anything more, she turned and hurried away.

After hearing that, I was completely disheartened. If Logan had turned down Hailey Wetmore, who was one of the most popular, attractive girls at our school, I knew I had no chance. As fast as I could, I turned to head in the opposite direction, away from Logan, but his voice stopped me in my tracks.

"Can you believe that? She tried to use the old book drop trick on me. How lame. Like I haven't seen that before."

I gulped. I didn't know what to do. Or say. Or think. I just stood there with a blank look on my face.

But then I realized something and it shook me to my core. He was talking to me. Logan McCoy, one of the best players on the football team, and one of the cutest boys at the school, was talking to me.

He continued. "I wish girls wouldn't be like that. I know I'm new here so it's not my place to be criticizing people, but I just wish they'd be more honest. If a girl wanted to meet me, I wish she'd just walk up and say hi."

I didn't know what else to do.

"Hi."

"That's more like it. You're Angel, right? Angel Williams?"

I almost passed out right there on the spot. I couldn't believe it. Not only was he talking to me, but he knew my name.

"Yeah."

"I saw you at the game last week. I asked around, and people told me who you were. They say you're a great softball player. They say you'll probably make the varsity team this year even though you're just a freshman."

"Really?" I liked the comment and wanted to learn more, especially who had said it and why, but softball had to wait. At that point in time, I had bigger fish to fry. I needed to focus on Logan and Logan alone. This was my big chance. I was actually talking to him and I needed to make the most of the opportunity.

But unfortunately, I couldn't think of anything to say. As such, I just stood there, completely silent, like a complete idiot. After a few seconds, I could feel my cheeks getting warm and I was clearly blushing.

"I should be going," Logan said. "Class is about to begin and since I'm new here, I don't want to be late. Need to make a good impression on the teachers, right? But anyway, I was wondering, and I hope you don't think this is too forward since we just met like thirty seconds ago, but I've been wanting to ask you ever since I saw you at the game if you wanted to go and do something. Like maybe grab some dinner or just something simple like coffee. Whatever you like is fine with me. I'm not picky."

My heart missed a beat. And when I say 'missed a beat' I mean 'missed fifty beats.' I couldn't believe what had happened. Had he actually asked me out? I knew I was dreaming. After all, nothing that good had ever happened to me in real life.

The only response I could muster was, "When?"

"Maybe tonight if you're free."

I was about to say yes but I remembered something.

"I thought you had to help your uncle tonight with chores."

Logan grinned. "I made that up. To be honest, I didn't want to go out with Bailey. I'm certain she's a really nice person but she's not my type. But I'd definitely like to go out with you if you're interested. Can you get free? I hear Starbucks is popular here in the Northwest. We could get a mocha or something."

I was so happy I couldn't speak and too in shock to even realize what was actually transpiring. My only response was an excited nod.

"Ok, good. I have practice right after school. Can I meet you after practice at the Starbucks that's across from the football field?"

I nodded. To be honest, I would have met him anywhere.

"Sweet. I'll see you then, Angel. And thanks, you've totally made my day."

He rushed off and I just continued standing there, rooted to my spot in the middle of the hallway for what seemed like an eternity. My head was spinning and my heart was on fire in my chest. I couldn't believe what had just happened. Much to my surprise and delight, I had gotten a date with Logan McCoy. And it got even better a few seconds later when Lea walked up. She had been standing in the distance, watching the whole thing from afar, and she looked as surprised as I did.

"OMG. You did it. You got a date with Logan McCoy. There's no doubt about it, no doubt at all. You're the coolest girl in the world."

I met him at Starbucks after his practice. I was nervous at first, and when I say nervous, I'm not kidding. My hands were shaking. I hid them behind my back so he couldn't see them. It was unbelievable, however, how quickly I settled down and felt at ease with him. He was really nice and soft spoken and gentle. And courteous. He ordered a pumpkin spice latte for me, which is one of my favorites, and he got a white chocolate mocha for himself, and we grabbed a couple of chairs in a corner and lounged around for hours. I told him about my life, as boring as it was, and he told me about his. He was from a small town about an hour west of Dallas called Huckstin.

"I've never heard of Huckstin before."

"No one has. It's a small place and I doubt it even appears on most maps. But it's nice in some ways. My dad is a mechanic and he has an auto shop in the downtown hub. He does really good business, especially in the spring and summer when the weather is good. I work at the shop with him when it's busy and he needs extra help. I'm actually pretty good at fixing cars, at least simple things, so if you ever need anything just give me the word."

I didn't have a car or even a driver's license but it didn't matter. So far, I liked what I had heard. Logan was cute, charming, good at football, and handy. It didn't get much better than that.

He went on to tell me about his family, how his parents had divorced when he had been six, and how his dad had been awarded custody of him, and how his dad had remarried a few years later and he now had two younger half-brothers named Hank and Billy Bob. Then we talked about what we liked and what we didn't, and I couldn't believe how much we had in common. We both loved Italian food, especially lasagna, with extra cheese, our favorite color was blue, our favorite band was Green Day, and our birthdays were both in October. His birthday was on October 1 and mine was on October 24.

The more we talked, the more I liked him. And when I say like, I mean like like, like how a girlfriend likes a boyfriend. Not like how a brother likes his sister. But there was one thing I was still curious about.

"Why did you move to the Northwest? And why by yourself, without your family? That seems a little odd."

For a brief second, his eyes got large. This was clearly a subject he didn't like to discuss too much. His voice was quiet as he gave me an explanation.

"I had an argument with my stepmother."

I raised an eyebrow.

"Actually," he continued. "I had several arguments with my stepmother."

"What do you mean?"

"She means well but she doesn't treat me the same as her sons, my half-brothers. She tries, I'll give her credit, but it just isn't meant to be. And it really upsets me sometimes. One night, right at the end of summer, we had a big argument and I got mad and called her a witch. So then my dad got really upset. Which is pretty unusual for him since he's chill most of the time. He told me to apologize but I refused."

"So he sent you to the Northwest?" I found that hard to believe. As far as solutions to problems went, it seemed way too drastic.

Logan laughed. "Of course not. Moving to the Northwest was my idea. My dad was completely against it at first. He was mad, don't get me wrong, especially since I wouldn't apologize, but he would never send me away because of it. He's not like that at all."

"So you wanted to come here?"

"Yeah. I've always liked my uncle and one time a few years back he floated the idea of me coming to stay with him for awhile, so I finally thought, *'What the heck?'* and I thought it would be good because it would give my stepmother and me some time to cool down. And I felt really bad for my dad."

"What do you mean?"

"My dad is in a bad situation. He has me from his first marriage and his other sons, my half-brothers, from his current marriage. Hank is five and Billy Bob is four. They're good kids most of the time, and we get along pretty well. Hank wants to be a football player like me when he's older. But my dad is always caught in the middle. My stepmother wants him to spend his time with Hank and Billy Bob since they're her sons and she gets really upset if he spends too much time with me. So he tries his best to balance his time between the three of us but it isn't easy, and sometimes I don't make things any easier on him, either, especially since I want him to spend the majority of his time with me. A few years back, I got really mad because he went to one of Hank's games instead of mine and I demanded he divorce her so he could spend more time with me, but of course he wouldn't do that and now looking back it was pretty stupid of me to say something like that because that wouldn't have been fair to him or to my younger brothers. It's just really complex. Blended families have endless issues. Anyway, my dad finally agreed to let me come up here and live with my uncle but only for a year. And I have to call him at least once a day but don't tell the guys on the football team about that or they'll think I'm a wuss and make fun of me."

I smiled. "Your secret is safe with me."

We stayed at Starbucks until it closed, talking nonstop the entire time, and never once did the smile leave my face.

September 22

There's no doubt about it. My older sister, Chloe, is the most annoying, inconsiderate, and obnoxious person on the planet. She's seventeen so she's two years older than me. She thinks she's so cool since she's a junior and I'm "just" a freshman and since she has a driver's license and I don't. In addition, her boyfriend is Caleb Davies, the star quarterback on the football team, so she's really popular and she goes to all of the school's dances and other cool activities. And if that isn't enough, she plays fastpitch, too, for an 18u team called the Washington Wildcats. Since she's older than me, she's bigger, stronger, faster, and more experienced, so she thinks she's better than me, but I don't buy it for a second.

Anyway, my team had a tournament this weekend in Everett, a city about fifteen miles north of Seattle. It was at a nice park on the west side of town and was an 18u tournament so it was for older teams but my team entered it anyway since we've been doing well lately and Coach Smith wanted to challenge us by putting us up against some stiff competition. Despite being the only 16u team participating, we started the weekend well and beat a team called the Pressure 4-0. We followed that performance by beating a team called the A's 5-4. But then the real action began.

We got to play Chloe's team.

True to character, Chloe made fun of me and taunted me before the game even started. "We'll try not to embarrass you little girls too much." She put special emphasis on the word 'little.'

She and her teammates laughed as they rounded up their softball bags and headed to their dugout.

I hate to admit it, but I was a little apprehensive. Chloe's team is really good and they win almost all of their games. And Chloe is their star pitcher so I knew it was going to be me against her, head-to-head, sooner or later.

We had never faced one another before, not in a game. Being sisters, we've practiced together forever, at McCall Park and in our back yard, but we had never had a game against one another until today.

"I heard your sister is really good," Lea said as we warmed up. I could see a look of concern in her eyes. "They say she throws really hard. And they say her changeup is nasty."

"She's okay, but nothing special. We can handle her."

Maybe not. Chloe was on fire to start the game, and she struck out our first six batters, including me. I went down swinging on three straight fastballs. The pitches sounded like explosions as they hit the catcher's mitt.

"Better luck next time," Chloe said as I walked back to the dugout. There was a smug smile on her face as she said it.

Luckily, our pitcher, Laura, was almost as good as Chloe and the game remained scoreless until I got my second at-bat in the fourth inning. This time, I did a little better and I fouled the first two pitches away.

Chloe grinned at me from her spot in the pitching circle. "Look at that. Someone finally showed up to play. Let's see how you can handle an inside pitch, little girl."

The next pitch was pure heat and it nailed me in the elbow. It hit me so hard my entire arm went numb for a couple of minutes. I couldn't even move my fingers. I shot Chloe a nasty look as the coaches examined me and made certain I was okay to continue.

Chloe acted like it was no big deal. "Shake it off, Angel. It's not that bad. It barely grazed you."

"BS," I responded, and I was really mad. It hurt like a beast, especially at first. "You did that on purpose. You hit me intentionally." I was about to say something more and I was even considering walking out to the pitching circle so I could say it to her face, but Blue interceded and sent me to first base.

Unfortunately, Chloe struck out the next batter and ended the inning, so we had to take the field.

Coach Smith greeted me in the dugout as I grabbed my glove and started to head to my position at short. "Are you certain you're okay? I can put in a sub for a couple of innings if you want. Give you a couple of minutes to recover."

I was still pretty mad at Chloe so my answer was blunt and not nearly as polite as normal. "I'm fine."

As far as I was concerned, I had some unfinished business and I needed to take care of it immediately. Someone needed some payback and I was going to give it to her.

It didn't take long for me to get my chance. Chloe was the leadoff batter and she hit a shot off of the outfield wall. Our center fielder, Kimi, grabbed the ball and whipped it to me at second, but Chloe got there first. The play wasn't even close but it didn't matter, not to me. I grabbed the ball out of the air and slapped the tag down anyway, as hard as I could, right in Chloe's face.

She pushed my glove away. "What the heck, Angel? Knock it off."

My answer was immediate. "You knock it off."

She tried to get up by I reached over and held her down. She retaliated and tried to force her way up, so I shoved her down again. Things were about to get really ugly but Homer, who had been watching the game attentively from his spot in the dugout, darted onto the field, got between us, and broke it up. He wasn't happy to see us fighting and he barked at us to let us know exactly what he thought of our behavior.

He wasn't the only one who was upset. Blue called our coaches over for a meeting at home plate.

"When I'm in charge, that type of behavior is unacceptable. I should eject both of them right now."

Chloe and I took a deep breath and glanced at our dad sitting in the stands. He didn't say anything but his face was red. Like everyone, he had watched the entire altercation and you didn't have to be a genius to figure out how he felt about it. We knew we were in deep trouble if we got ejected. There would be lengthy groundings for sure.

Luckily, we didn't get ejected. Blue decided a stern warning was enough and the game continued from there. The Wildcats got a run that inning and another the next, and they were leading 2-0 when I got my final at-bat in the top of the seventh inning.

Chloe had a smile on her face and she rocked back and forth on her heels as I took my place in the batter's box. She had us right where she wanted us. She had the lead and she only needed three more outs to finish us off.

I dug my cleats into the dirt, tapped my bat on the plate, and took a deep breath. This was my last chance to prove myself. I needed to grit my teeth and do it.

But it wasn't going to be easy. The first pitch was a nasty riseball and I missed it by a mile. As was so often the case when dealing with riseballs, I swung under it. Way under. The second pitch was a curveball, down and away. The third, fourth, and fifth pitches were fastballs and I fouled them all away. I barely got a piece of the last one. For a brief second I thought I was a goner but I nicked it and somehow managed to stay alive.

The next pitch was a changeup, and a nasty one, at least fifteen miles per hour slower than the previous pitch, but it didn't fool me at all. I kept my hands back as long as I could, then swung with everything I had. I hit it hard, straight up the middle, and it nailed Chloe and ricocheted to the side.

That'll teach her, I thought as I ran to first. *She won't hit me with a pitch again.*

But then something unexpected happened. Out of the corner of my eye, I saw Homer leave his place in the dugout and run straight toward the pitching circle. That was strange and immediately caught my attention because even though Homer was new to the softball world, he knew to stay off of the field until a play was completely over. But then I figured out what had happened. Homer had run to the pitching circle because he had realized Chloe was hurt. And she was hurt badly. She was on her back, in a really awkward position with her legs bent at the knees and pinned under her body. Her arms were sprawled to her sides and her face was covered in blood, and it was obvious she was unconscious since she wasn't moving at all. I hadn't realized it at first because things had happened so fast, but the ball had hit her straight in the face.

I nearly freaked out as I realized what I had done.

I had killed my sister.

Luckily, she wasn't actually dead but she didn't start moving until Homer got to her and put a paw on her shoulder. I was instantly relieved to see her regain consciousness and start moving around, but terrified by what happened next. The minute her eyes opened, her entire body began to shake like she was having a convulsion, and she screamed in pain so loudly it could be heard by players on adjacent fields. Their games came to a screeching halt as everyone looked over and tried to figure out what had happened. Chloe didn't calm down and her screaming and shaking didn't stop until the Wildcats' coach and my dad got to her. My dad was nothing but a blur as he raced from his spot in the stands to the pitching circle; I've never seen him move so fast in my entire life. In an attempt to calm her down he grabbed her by the sides of the face and forced her to look right at him.

"It's going to be okay, Chloe. You're going to be fine. Look at me and take a deep breath."

It took a few tries and he had to repeat his words several times but it finally worked. She stopped shaking and just laid there as my dad and the Wildcats' coach attended to her injury. She had a nasty gouge on her forehead where the ball had hit her, so my dad wrapped it up the best he could to control the bleeding, which was showing no signs of stopping any time soon. It was a complete mess and he didn't have enough medical wrap so he turned to Homer.

"Sorry, fella. I need to borrow this."

He took Homer's bandana from his neck and wrapped it around Chloe's head. In no time, it was soaked with blood but it helped a lot. The Wildcats' coach asked Chloe how she was doing but she was still crying too hard to give a coherent answer.

By this time, I was a complete wreck. I was crying almost as hard as her. Tears flooded my cheeks. I never meant to hurt her so badly. I wouldn't have minded a small injury, like a bruise on her arm or a welt on her leg, but nothing like this. This was way too serious. From the dugout, Coach Smith saw me and ran over to comfort me.

"She'll be okay, Angel. Hang in there."

"It's totally my fault."

"No, it isn't. These things happen on occasion. You know what we always say. There's nothing soft about softball."

I appreciated the attempt but his words didn't make me feel much better, if at all. An ambulance arrived a few minutes later, its lights flashing and its siren blazing. There were three paramedics and they examined Chloe carefully, placed her on a stretcher, and carried her off of the field. My dad and I followed them and climbed inside the ambulance to ride with them to the nearest hospital. One of the paramedics, who was a tall man with red hair, was about to close the door when Homer jumped inside.

The paramedic looked at me. It was clear he didn't know what to do. "We don't usually allow dogs in the ambulance."

"He's a special dog. He goes where we go."

Not knowing what else to do, the paramedic shrugged, closed the door, and off we went. I turned to Chloe and could barely control myself.

"I'm sorry. I didn't mean to do it. I was just trying so hard. I thought it was a good hit."

Chloe still looked like a wreck but she had calmed down a lot and was only crying a little. "It was, Angel. It was a good hit."

Her response surprised me so much I couldn't even respond. I just sat there with a blank look on my face. Luckily, she elaborated.

"That's what dad taught us, right? Hit the ball up the middle. You did your job and you did it well."

I didn't know what to say. I appreciated the compliment, especially since it was coming from her and especially after all that had happened, but I was sick to my stomach and for a few minutes I thought I was going to vomit right there in the ambulance. Much to my relief, I didn't, and we arrived at the hospital a few minutes later. The paramedics wheeled Chloe through the emergency room, down a hallway, and into a room for a formal examination and a CAT scan. Luckily, everything went fine and the CAT scan revealed no internal damage or bleeding of any type. The doctor, who was an older man with dark gray hair, stitched up Chloe's forehead. It took twenty-five stitches to complete the job.

"I want to see you for a check-up in a couple of days. And no softball or anything physical until then. Understood?"

Chloe nodded. "I have a terrible headache. It feels like a bomb went off in my head."

"That's to be expected after what you went through. I'll give you something for it. It should go away in a few hours."

I let out a huge sigh. I've never felt so relieved in my entire life. Like most older sisters, Chloe can be a real witch at times but, regardless, I wanted her to recover and return to normal as soon as possible. As soon as we got home, I made her a bowl of minestrone, which is her favorite, and Homer and I climbed into bed with her. We surfed the internet together using her laptop computer. After an hour, Cinnamon saw us in her bedroom and he didn't want Homer to get all of the attention so he joined us, and it was pretty crowded with all four of us in that bed at once, but it was actually pretty nice, and it was the most time Chloe and I have spent together in ages.

I guess it's true what they say. Sometimes bad things can be good things in a weird sort of way. Earlier in the day, during our game, Chloe and I had been bickering like a couple of petty preschoolers. But now, just a few hours later, that bickering was gone and as far as I was concerned, it wasn't going to return for a long, long time.

September 23

My dad is a professor. He teaches history at the University of Washington and he's taught there for as long as I remember. But he's not a normal professor, at least as far as I can tell. He doesn't come home and read history books, or magazine articles, or anything intellectual like that at all. Instead, he spends most of his time playing *Rock Band*. And he's pretty good at it, especially when he plays guitar or drums, but he sucks at keyboard. Chloe and I join in on occasion and I play bass. Chloe likes to sing so she's our front man. She has a pretty voice, especially on songs with a lot of melody, and she's really good with her runs. Homer is our manager and Cinnamon is the president of our fan club. We formed our own imaginary band called *Crazy Crew*. Today, since Chloe is still recovering from her concussion and can't do much, we spent most of the day playing and it was really fun. But the only bad thing was we spent a lot of time arguing over what song to play next. My dad loves the hard stuff, especially death, thrash, and speed metal. Ugh. His favorite bands are Five Finger Death Punch (ouch), Godsmack (good lord), and Korn. I've never understood why a band would want to be called

Korn, let alone why they would spell their name with a K. It hurts my ears to think about it. Chloe, Homer, Cinnamon, and I, by contrast, like 'normal' music, and our favorite artists are Green Day, Katy Perry, and Snoop Dogg. And luckily, since there are more of us than my dad, we outvote him, so we only have to listen to his devil worshipping music on occasion.

September 24

Just my luck. Coach Smith got fired today. Our dads finally got sick of him and got rid of him and I guess I should have seen it coming. After all, the dads always think they can do a better job than the coach no matter how hard the coach tries and no matter how well he does. But that wasn't the real problem, at least not in this case. Our dads were still upset about how our previous season had ended, and for good reason. Coach Smith, like all coaches, always says softball is "all about the girls" but everyone knows it isn't. It's about the coaches. And all they really care about are their own daughters (how much playing time they get) and winning. A perfect example of that happened last year when my team flew to California to play in a tournament in Los Angeles. My teammate, Olivia Sanchez, was in a batting slump so Coach Smith hardly played her at all during the trip, so her parents spent all of that money to fly to California, and they rented a hotel room and a car, basically for nothing. One night, Olivia got so upset she started to cry. We girls tried to make her feel better but Coach Smith didn't care and he spent the rest of the night sitting in the hotel's lobby, in the bar, drinking beer and bragging about how his brilliant tactical decisions had led us to a huge victory earlier in the day.

A second and even more troubling incident happened at the final tournament of the season in Wenatchee. Another one of my teammates, a girl named Kristin King, broke her arm diving to make a catch. It was a spectacular play, one of the best I've ever seen, and it won the game for us. Of course Coach Smith was happy about that. He even called the emergency room as they were doing Kristin's x-rays to see how she was doing. But since it was the final tournament of the season, Kristin didn't have enough time to heal fully before the commencement of the following season, so her arm was still in a cast and she couldn't do tryouts with the rest of us. Coach Smith cut her from the team as a result.

So I'm not really too upset about him getting fired. In many ways, he was a jerk, especially the way he treated Olivia and Kristin. But here's what I'm upset about. His replacement is my greatest nightmare. It's my dad. The other dads decided my dad was the best choice to be the new coach, so he's it. And now he doesn't want the other dads to think he's favoring his daughter in any way so he's being twice as hard on me as he is the other girls. Today, at practice, Kimi let a ground ball go through her legs and he called out, "That's okay, Kimi, you'll get the next one." A few minutes later, I let one get past me and he yelled out, "Keep your mitt in the dirt, Angel. You know better than that."

And if that wasn't bad enough, when we girls were sitting in the dugout, taking a water break, Kimi had the nerve to say, "I'm so glad your dad is the new coach, Angel. He's the nicest guy in the world."

I was flabbergasted. "You've got to be kidding me. My dad is a pain in the butt."

"No way. Your dad is so cool. He's not like my dad at all. My dad is a beast. He's in a bad mood all day long."

Lea, who was sitting on the bench next to us, laughed. "You two don't know what you're talking about. My dad is the worst of all. He yells at me all of the time and he never listens to me at all."

I shook my head and I didn't care what they said. I've met both of their dads many times over the years. Kimi's dad's name is Craig and Lea's dad's name is Dale and they're two of the nicest guys I've ever met. My dad, by contrast, can be a real jerk at times, especially the time when I was eight and I spilled paint all over the kitchen floor. I know he told me to be careful and make certain the lid was on the can tightly before I picked it up, but he still didn't need to be such a creep about it afterward. Now that he's the new coach, this could be a long and extremely frustrating year for me.

But one good thing did come of the coaching change. On the drive home from practice, I asked my dad about Kristin and he said to call her and get her back on the team. He didn't care that we already had a full roster of twelve girls, and he said it would be fine to play the rest of the season with thirteen. So I did and Kristin officially became my teammate again, which made me really happy. Kristin is a nice girl and it was completely unfair what happened to her, so it was good to see things finally made right.

September 27

Today I went to the football game, to see Logan play, and just like the previous week, he was amazing. Our game was against a school called Snohomish and it was a road game so Lea's mom gave us a ride and dropped us off at Snohomish's stadium, which is in the downtown area, not too far from the high school itself. There were three of us total: Kimi, Lea, and me. We cheered as the game began and our team wasted little time getting on the scoreboard. Our quarterback, Caleb, threw a pass to one of our receivers, a senior named Kellen Allen, and he ran eighty yards for the opening score. It was a great play and was quite exciting, especially when he dove for the goal line, but it was nothing compared to what Logan did a few minutes later. He took a handoff from Caleb, rushed through the line, sidestepped a would-be tackler, and dragged three more defenders into the endzone for a touchdown. All three defenders were bigger and heavier than Logan, by quite a bit, but they couldn't stop him anyway. He was too strong and too determined.

There's no doubt about it.

He's perfect. In every way.

September 29

Until this year, I had never played for the same team for more than a season. Every year, something always happened and I moved on to a new team. My first year, when I played for the King County Khaos, my dad got in an argument with the coach so we decided to switch to another team, which was actually a good thing since my new team, the Eastside Angels, turned out to be much better than the Khaos. At first, the Angels seemed perfect, like they always do, but it was always kind of weird since my name is Angel and I played for a team called the Angels. That got a few laughs during my tenure with them. Unfortunately, things soured by the end of the season because my coach got a divorce, started spending an inordinate amount of time with his new girlfriend, started showing up late to games, and started skipping practices. He'd leave things up to the assistant coaches, which they didn't mind, but you can imagine how well that went over with my dad. So I moved on to the Seattle Softball Club and that was a really good fit for a while, and it was definitely one of the best teams I've ever been on, but it disbanded after a year when most of the girls, for various reasons, decided they wanted to play for someone else. So I moved on to my current team, the Seattle Sky, which still seems pretty good despite the recent coaching change, but I'm not getting my hopes up because I know how it works. Sooner or later the girls will start bickering or the dads will get upset and on I'll go from here. I don't really like it, I'd prefer to stay on the same team indefinitely, but what can I do? It is what it is.

Anyway, today was a stressful day. My team had a tournament in south Seattle at a park not too far from the airport and my final game was against one of my old teams, the Eastside Angels. Some of my former teammates are still on the Angels and several of them are still my friends. It was good to see them again but at the same time I felt like I needed to do really well against them. After all, who wants to play poorly against her friends?

The Angels' pitcher is a girl I've known since kindergarten. Her name is Ashley Martinez and she goes to my school. We're pretty good friends but we're über competitive and we've had some heated arguments regarding who is the superior player. As such, I knew I better not strike out against her or I'd hear about it for sure at school on Monday morning, if not sooner.

Unfortunately, the game didn't start well. Ashley got two quick strikes on me, both with fastballs, then finished me off with a nasty slider. It was down in the dirt and I knew I shouldn't swing at it but I couldn't help myself and chased after it anyway.

Ashley grinned at me as I headed back to the dugout. "You can't get them all, Angel."

She was being nice on the outside but I knew what she was really doing. She was mocking me.

As I sat in the dugout, I was fuming. I was absolutely furious at myself. Ashley wasn't even that good. Over the years, I had faced a bazillion pitchers who were better than her and I had done fine against them. How in the world had she struck me out?

My next at-bat came in the third inning. This time I did a little better, but not much. I hit the first pitch really hard but straight at the Angels' shortstop, Brooke Conrad, whom is another friend of mine. It's never a good idea to hit a ball at Brooke, because she's so good nothing gets by her. She reached out and caught the ball with ease.

Ashley smiled at me again. "Better luck next time."

I'm going to be blunt; at that point, she was really starting to get on my nerves. I needed to get a hit during my final at-bat or the game would turn into a complete disaster. Unfortunately, and despite my best efforts, it wasn't meant to be. I fouled two pitches straight back, then struck out swinging at a curveball. The minute I got back to the dugout, Homer looked at me and shook his head in disgust. Even he was disappointed with my performance.

Ashley sent me a text during the drive home. It read, "Don't worry about today's game, Angel. We all stink it up on occasion."

I deleted her message without responding. I'll get her back the next time we play. Just you wait and see.

October 2

I was sitting at my desk in my bedroom working on some homework, when I got this bizarre feeling, as though someone was watching me. I looked over and saw Homer and Cinnamon on my bed, but it wasn't either of them because they were both sound asleep. Homer was snoring softly, like usual. So I looked across to the far side of the room and there was Chloe, standing in the doorway. Much to my delight, she was recovering nicely from her injury and most of the swelling in her face and forehead had gone away. But there was something odd about her. She was staring right at me with a weird look on her face.

"Is it true?"

I had no idea what she was talking about so I said nothing.

"Is it true you're seeing Logan McCoy?"

My heart raced the minute she said Logan's name.

"We're not really seeing each other. I don't think. But we did go out. It was nothing fancy but it was nice and he did tell me he wanted to go out again."

Chloe smiled. "Don't be so modest, Angel. You've got that boy eating out of the palm of your hand. He's totally gaga over you."

My heart stopped. Did Chloe know something I didn't? Something about Logan?

"Caleb and Logan have been hanging out a lot lately," she explained. "I know it's kind of unusual, since Caleb is a senior and Logan is a sophomore, but I guess that's how football players are; they don't care what grade you're in as long as you're good. Anyway, we all went to dinner last night, after their practice, and Caleb invited Logan. We're all sitting around talking and Logan said something about this girl he went out with, a freshman who is a star softball player and is really cute. He said he really liked her and said she was as sweet as watermelon wine, which I guess is how they say something is good in Texas. Anyway, he asked if any of us knew her and Caleb said, 'What's her name?'"

I couldn't believe what I was hearing. It was too good to be true. "He said me?"

"Of course he said it was you. But then he got really embarrassed because everyone started laughing. They knew who you were and they knew you were my sister, but Logan was clueless until they told him."

I hated the thought of them making fun of him. "They didn't give him a hard time, did they?"

"Of course they did; they're guys. They tease each other about everything. But it wasn't a big deal because they really like him. And that's pretty impressive since he just moved here so people don't know him too well. After hearing who he was interested in, I decided I better spend a little time with him myself, one on one, to find out what he's like and all. After all, I can't have some weirdo hanging out with my baby sister."

My eyes got big with alarm. Chloe had talked to Logan? About me?

"It was a little awkward at first. He was pretty embarrassed. And he says he didn't catch on that we're sisters since he says we don't look too much alike."

It's true. Chloe and I are both tall and thin, but our similarities end there. She has blue eyes, whereas mine are deep brown (I prefer the term chocolate). And her hair is much longer and lighter than mine. Overall, I'm a lot prettier than her but don't tell her or it'll just make her feel bad.

She continued. "Things got much better as time went on. And it's undeniable. He's really nice. And his accent is adorable. It's mesmerizing just listening to it. He's from some place in Texas I've never heard of before."

I remembered it instantly. "Huckstin."

"Yeah, that sounds right, I think. Anyway, there's no doubt about it. He's crazy about you."

"Really? What'd he say?"

"He wouldn't say much once he found out you were my sister. He knew I'd tell you. But let's just say I could tell. He had that look in his eyes."

"That look?"

"Yeah, you know. Every time I mentioned your name his eyes sparkled. And he wanted to know everything about you. What softball team you played for, how long you've played, blah, blah, blah. I don't know what you did, Angel, but you got him. Hook, line, and sinker."

I sat there, completely speechless. I couldn't believe what I had heard but I knew one thing for sure. I wanted to hear more. Luckily, Chloe continued.

"The other guys think it's hilarious."

"What?"

"Caleb and Logan, the star players on the football team, are dating sisters. And we're both star softball players, at least according to them. They think it's cosmic or something."

I had never heard that expression before. "Cosmic?"

"Meant to be. And I have to agree, if nothing else, it is pretty funny. It caught me completely off guard. I always knew you had potential, Angel, and I knew you'd find a good boyfriend sooner or later, but I didn't think you'd do this well. As far as I can tell, this Logan is as close to perfect as you can get. He's a gem."

She turned to leave, but then stopped briefly to say one final thing.

"It's hard to believe. One day, my baby sister could be as popular as me."

With a chuckle, she turned and left.

I was in seventh heaven the rest of the night. I couldn't sit still and I never did finish my homework. I couldn't believe it, but my dreams were coming true.

Logan liked me.

October 3

My dad is a beast. At practice, he's still giving me a rough time and he's definitely being harsher on me than the rest of the girls. He made me run an extra lap today because I missed a fly ball. It's true I was daydreaming about Logan and that's the reason I bombed the play, but still, that's no reason to get all fussy and single me out. The other girls, especially Lea, miss fly balls all the time and he doesn't make them run extra laps. Quite to the contrary, this was his response after a ball hit Lea's mitt and deflected to the side.

"Good effort, Lea. You'll get the next one."

Yeah, right. The next one was a grounder and she let it go right through her legs.

On the drive home, I was pretty fed up and was about to give him an earful, but then I decided to bite my tongue and let it go. He was in a good mood since, to him, it had been a "productive" practice, and I didn't want to ruin the moment with an argument. And besides, if there is one thing I learned a long time ago, dealing with parents is tricky, especially when your father is as pig-headed as mine, so I have to choose my battles wisely. I have a finite amount of energy and I can't go around wasting it on little things. And my dad is new to this coaching thing so hopefully things will change and he'll start treating me more fairly soon. But if he doesn't, I promise, he will feel my wrath.

October 4

Angel Williams.

I've never really liked my name. The Angel part is okay, since, well, who doesn't like angels, but Williams is so plain. So common. I might as well be named Angel Smith, Angel Jones, or Angel Adams.

Angel Dell Williams.

Ugh. I've never liked my middle name at all. No disrespect to my grandmother, who is my namesake, but it's too old-fashioned. Forget I even mentioned it.

Angel McCoy.

That sounds a lot better. It's exotic, and catchy, and it has a definite flair to it. I like how it looks. I like how McCoy has a lowercase C right before the uppercase C.

Logan and Angel McCoy.

That sounds exquisite. It rolls off the tongue. It's definitely meant to be.

October 5

Today my team had a tournament in Mount Vernon, a city about an hour's drive north of Seattle. It was an 18u tournament, for older teams, but it started well. Our first game was against a team from Oregon called the Portland Pioneers and we won 4-3. I went two for three with two singles and I made a couple of nice plays in the field, including a running catch to end the third inning. Our second game was against a team from Yakima called the Yellow Jackets. They wear these awful, yellow uniforms with horizontal black stripes. They are the brightest uniforms I've ever seen, and I had to put my sunglasses on just to look at them. The game went well and we won 5-4. I went one for three with a double.

But that was the end of the fun. Our third and final game was against a team called Stanwood Fastpitch, or SFP for short, and their pitcher, Kaitlyn Kingsbury, is really mean. She likes to throw brushback pitches for the fun of it. In case you don't know, a brushback pitch is a pitch that is thrown high and tight, missing the batter's head by inches. Brushback pitches are thrown to scare and intimidate the batter, and it was working. Kaitlyn's pitches were absolutely nasty and were scaring the you-know-what out of us. We hadn't gotten a single hit through the first four innings, and one of her pitches missed my helmet by a hair. My dad got so frustrated he called a timeout and challenged Blue.

"This needs to stop, right now. She's throwing at my batters."

Blue shrugged. "There's nothing I can do. Brushback pitches are legal as long as she doesn't hit the batter."

Not knowing what else to do, my dad returned to the dugout and the game continued from there. Before we knew it, we were losing 2-0.

But then everything changed. Kaitlyn made a mistake. Between innings, she walked over to the stands and spoke to Chloe. Chloe's team, the Wildcats, had the day off, so she was spending the day watching my games. Actually, she was spending most of her time texting, but she'd look up on occasion, especially when it was my turn to bat.

"I haven't seen you for a while," Kaitlyn said. "How's it going?"

Chloe and Kaitlyn used to be good friends back when they were younger. Kaitlyn used to come over to our house regularly, sometimes for sleepovers. But things soured a year ago when they had a fight over Caleb. Caleb had originally been Kaitlyn's boyfriend but he broke up with her so he could start seeing Chloe.

"Good," Chloe responded. "How about you?"

"Not bad. You still playing for the Wildcats?"

Chloe nodded. They were both being cordial but there was still some obvious bad blood between them. I could feel the tension from ten feet away.

"How are the mighty Wildcats doing these days?"

"Not too bad. And you?"

Kaitlyn shrugged. "Same old, same old. You know how it is. They've got us playing these younger teams a lot lately and it's a complete waste of my time. I'll be amazed if I break a sweat today. All of these young teams suck, including this one. That dog they've got for a mascot is cute, but the rest of the team is worthless. There's not a good player in the bunch."

Chloe raised an eyebrow. "What about the shortstop? She looks pretty good."

Kaitlyn shrugged. "Average at best."

Chloe chuckled. "It was good seeing you again, Kaitlyn, but I gotta go. I've got some unfinished business to take care of."

She got up, headed back to our car in the nearby parking lot, and unloaded her softball bag. Since she wasn't playing today, I'm not certain why she brought it along, but after I found out what she was going to do, I was grateful. She carried it into our dugout, plopped it down on the bench next to Homer, and turned to my dad.

"Do you have a spare jersey?"

"A couple. They're in the equipment bag over there. Why?"

"I need to bring Kaitlyn down a peg or two. So I'm pitching from now on. Where's the ball?"

Every head in the dugout turned as one. I couldn't believe what I had just heard. Chloe had never played for us before. Technically, most of the time she couldn't since she was an older player, but today was an exception since we were playing in an 18u tournament.

"You're playing for us?"

"Only on one condition. Every girl on the team is going to go all-out from here on. Understood? I'm sick of Kaitlyn and her prissy attitude. And I'm especially sick of those brushbacks. Are you with me?"

We cheered. Homer barked. And we charged onto the field like a team reborn. We weren't afraid of Kaitlyn anymore. Now that we had Chloe pitching for us, we knew the tables had turned and we had a chance to win.

Chloe did not disappoint. She was still changing into her uniform as she headed to the pitching circle, and she had to wear a face mask to comply with her doctor's orders, but once the inning started, she was all business. She was absolutely on fire. Being her sister, I've known her forever but I've never seen her throw like that before. Her pitches were exploding in our catcher's mitt. The SFP batters were completely overwhelmed. All three of them struck out the first inning, and two of three the second.

In the meantime, we scored three runs. Kaitlyn was clearly rattled and she couldn't believe Chloe was pitching for us. The velocity of her pitches dipped significantly. Lea started things off with a single, Laura walked, I hit a single to load the bases, and Chloe followed with a massive triple off of the outfield wall that scored all three of us. Chloe hit it so hard I thought it was going to be a grand slam, but alas not quite. Regardless, it gave us the lead, 3-2, and we held onto it until the final batter of the final inning.

And then the real showdown began.

The grudge match of the century.

It was Kaitlyn's turn to bat.

Chloe versus Kaitlyn. Head-to-head.

Chloe's first pitch was so fast I could barely see it. From my position at short, it was a nothing more than a yellow blur. And it missed Kaitlyn's head by a centimeter. Maybe less. It was so close Kaitlyn's knees buckled and she fell to the ground in an attempt to get away from it. She was furious as she got back up.

"You did that on purpose."

Chloe grinned. "It's not so fun when they come at you. Is it?"

Kaitlyn dusted herself off, picked up her bat, and the battle waged on from there. The next pitch was straight down the middle for strike one, and the second was pure heat for strike two. Chloe tried to finish her off with a nasty changeup, but Kaitlyn fought it off and fouled it to the side. Chloe went back to her heat, but

Kaitlyn fouled the pitch away, and the next one, and the next, and the next.

It was a battle of epic proportions. Chloe and Kaitlyn had disliked one another for a while and neither girl was going to back down, not for a second. And, even though I didn't want to, I had to give Kaitlyn credit because she was a good batter. Chloe's pitches were so nasty they would have destroyed an average batter, but somehow Kaitlyn managed to stay alive, and she was really making Chloe work. I could see a layer of sweat forming on Chloe's brow as she threw pitch after pitch after pitch.

And then it happened. Kaitlyn finally got one of Chloe's pitches into play. She didn't hit it well, it was really nothing more than a weak blooper, but it was big trouble because it was hit over our third baseman's head but way too shallow for our left fielder to get to.

So there was only one player left who had a chance. Me. I darted from my position at short and dove as far as I could. It was probably the best dive I've ever made, completely outstretched as far as I could go, and I hit the ground so hard I didn't even feel the ball as it entered my mitt. At first, I didn't even know I had it, but as I lay there on the ground, face down on my stomach, I heard my teammates cheering and Homer barking triumphantly.

Chloe was the first player to get to me. She helped me up and patted me on the back.

"Thanks, Angel. I really wanted that one."

My response was immediate. "You helped us. I thought I'd return the favor."

From the dugout, my dad smiled. Like all dads, he liked it when his girls got along.

We won 3-2.

October 6

Today was a scary day. Logan had another game so of course I went. It was against a high school called Mariner and everything was going smoothly at first. We jumped to a big lead when Caleb completed a pair of touchdown passes to the big receivers, the ones that start each play on the line. I think they call them tightbacks or cornerends or something like that. Anyway, Logan added to the lead by scoring a touchdown of his own. And, like normal, it was a sweet play. Caleb handed him the ball, but he was in big trouble at first because a defender slipped through the line and barreled down on him. Somehow, miraculously, he pulled himself free and darted to the side, and it was off to the races from there. He turned the corner and rambled along the sideline for fifty yards. The defenders finally caught up to him and dragged him down from behind, but not until he had crossed the goal line. Everyone in the stands went crazy, and the cheerleaders, except Hailey Wetmore, did their jumps, kicks, and backflips.

But the fun, especially for me, ended in the fourth quarter. We were leading 24-0 and it was clear we were going to cruise to another easy victory. And if that wasn't good enough, we were threatening to score again. We had the ball and it was second down on Mariner's sixteen-yard line. Caleb tossed the ball to Logan, and Logan raced through the line, but a defender grabbed him by an arm, and another grabbed him by the waist, and two more piled on top of him. They went down in a heap at the five-yard line. I cheered because it was a first down, but then I noticed something was wrong. The audience had gone quiet and the cheerleaders had dropped to a knee. One of the players wasn't getting up and much to my chagrin it was one of the players who was wearing an orange and black jersey.

My heart stopped when I realized who it was. It was Logan. He was lying there, on the field where he had fallen. He was moving a little, but he was clearly in a lot of pain and he was holding his left knee with one hand. The referees blew their whistles and waved their arms to indicate a timeout, and our trainers and coaches ran onto the field to help him.

It only lasted a few minutes but it seemed like an eternity. At one point, I looked over and I saw Chloe in the bleachers a few rows down, with her friends. She looked up at me with a comforting, reassuring look on her face.

"Don't worry. He'll be okay."

Luckily, and much to my relief, he was. After working with his knee for a few minutes, the trainers helped him up and he was able to walk off of the field by himself without much help. Apparently, he had twisted his knee badly, but not bad enough to cause any serious or lasting damage. Our coaches, however, had seen more than enough and they weren't going to take any additional chances with their star running back, so they took his helmet from him and he didn't play any more for the remainder of the game.

Which was perfectly fine with me. After all, I like this football thing, and having a potential boyfriend who is a football player is nice, but why does the darn sport have to be so rough? If I were in charge, I'd make a new rule so only one player could attempt to tackle Logan at a time.

But then again, if I did that, they'd never have a chance.

October 7

Logan came to my game today. He had a slight limp from his knee injury but all-in-all he was okay and he told me to not worry about him.

"I've been injured before. It's no big deal. I'll be back to full speed in no time, just you wait and see."

He always has a smile on his face and such a good attitude. I could learn a lot from him. Some days, for no reason at all, I wake up in a bad mood. On those days, Chloe always tells me to "turn my frown upside down" but all that does is put me in an even worse mood.

Anyway, I was ecstatic because he was here to watch me, but I was nervous, too, big time. Normally, I was the one watching him while he played, not the other way around. But now that he was here, I wanted to impress him and I wanted to impress him big. I wanted to show him how good I was and how perfect a couple we could be. He was a star football player. I was a star softball player. It doesn't get much better than that.

But it didn't start well. Our game was against a team from British Columbia called the Vancouver Victory. They have a really cool logo on their uniforms that has a pair of overlapping Vs and a red maple leaf. The leadoff batter hit a grounder right at me, which normally would have been a nice, routine play, and one ive done a million times over the years, but I did the dumbest thing imaginable. I didn't get my mitt all of the way down into the dirt and I let the ball go right through my legs for an error.

Wonderful, I thought. Whenever I went and watched Logan play, he always did so well and put on such a great show for me. But now that he had come to watch me play, what had I done? I had messed up the whole thing miserably. I was so embarrassed I couldn't even look his way.

But he seemed unfazed. "It's okay, Angel. You'll get the next one."

Luckily, I did. It took a couple of batters but I got a much-needed shot at redemption. The Victory's second baseman hit a ball to my right, and she hit it really hard. Normally, I prefer to move over and get my body in front of hits like that, but it was moving too quickly so I reached over and grabbed it with my backhand, which has never been one of my strengths, then turned and fired it to first for an out.

This time, I was willing to shoot a glance at Logan in the stands and, as expected, he was nothing but smiles.

His smile got even bigger in the bottom half of the inning. It was my turn to bat. The Victory's pitcher was a tall, lean girl with dark hair that came all of the way down to her waist. Her first couple of pitches had great velocity but were slightly outside, so I let them go for balls, but then she tried to mix things up by throwing a changeup straight down the middle of the plate. It was a decent pitch since it was at least fifteen miles per hour slower than its predecessors, but it didn't fool me for a second. I timed my swing perfectly and lined the ball past her for a single. Everyone, including Logan, cheered as I stepped on first base.

But the highlight of the game came in the sixth inning. At that point, I was two for two with a pair of singles, so I was having a solid game and I was feeling pretty good about my performance. As the game had progressed, my confidence had improved and Logan seemed impressed so I was happy, but not completely. In my opinion, Logan deserved a lot more than singles. He deserved something big. Something with some power.

So I went up to the plate with a mission, with one thing, and only one thing, on my mind. I was going to give the ball a one-way ticket to the outfield fence. And boy did I. It took three pitches but I hit the ball so hard it flew all of the way to the deepest part of the outfield. The centerfielder made a running stab at it but missed it by a foot or so, and before she could recover and throw it back to the infield, I was standing at third base with a two-run triple.

Logan was all smiles.

And so was I.

October 9

Today was one of the greatest days ever. Logan came over for dinner and I was pretty nervous at first, since this was the first time I've ever had a boy come over for dinner, and my dad always worries me when it comes to boys. Like most men who have teenage daughter, he's not a big fan of them. Remarkably, however, it went really well. My dad liked Logan right from the start, and he loved the fact Logan was a running back, just like he had been when he had played at Monroe a hundred years ago. To be honest, I didn't even know they had football back in those days and it must have been when they wore those strange, leather helmets, but anyway, they did. My dad's actually pretty old, almost forty-five, but he still has a good memory for a man his age and he can remember every detail of every game just like it was yesterday. Which is actually pretty odd since he can never remember anything else, including my mom's birthday or their anniversary, and he got in a lot of trouble this past year because of it, but that's a story for another day. Anyway, he and Logan exchanged stories all night and my dad was really fascinated with the fact Logan played football in Texas.

"What's it like in Texas? I've heard school ball is huge there."

Logan nodded. "It is. In some of the smaller towns like Huckstin the entire town shuts down on Friday night and everyone goes to the game. And when I say everyone, I don't just mean the students and their parents, like up here in the Northwest. I mean everyone. Little kids, grandparents, shop owners, the mayor, everyone."

My dad smiled. "No wonder there are so many great players from Texas. And no wonder the Longhorns are so good every year."

I wasn't certain who the Longhorns were, maybe the NFL team from San Antonio or Austin, but to be honest, I didn't really care. As long as my dad and Logan were getting along, that was all that mattered to me.

"Do you go to the games, Mister Williams?" Logan asked.

"You can call me Dan."

Chloe, my mom, and I shot glances at one another. That was a good sign. My dad would only let a boy call him by his first name if he really liked him. Even Chloe's boyfriend, Caleb, wasn't allowed to call him by first name, at least not yet.

My dad took a bite of his dinner and then continued. "I used to go but I stopped a ways back. I got so busy with other things. Family, softball, and all. But it would be nice. I definitely miss those old games."

"You should come. We have a big one this week against a school called Arlington. I don't know much about them but they're supposed to be really good and the other guys want to beat them pretty bad."

My dad's eyes got big the minute he heard the name. "I hate Arlington. They were our rivals back when I played. We lost to them my first two years, but finally beat them the third year. Man that was a good game. Do me a favor and show no mercy, Logan."

Logan's response was immediate. "Yes, sir. I mean, Dan."

My dad loaded his plate up with some mashed potatoes. "You're a good kid, Logan. And maybe you're right. Maybe I should come and watch that game on Friday. I wouldn't mind seeing my old Bearcats kick some Eagle butt."

Dinner was great, especially since the interaction between Logan and my dad went so well, but the highlight of the night, by far, was afterward, when Homer and I walked Logan out to his car in the driveway. It was actually his uncle's car, some type of Mustang, but his uncle let him borrow it for the night.

"Your family is really nice, Angel. I really like your dad. He's a nice guy. He reminds me a lot of my dad."

"He has his moments. But trust me, you don't want to be around him on a bad day, like last semester when I got my progress report in Washington state history. That was not good."

Logan chuckled. But then there was a brief, awkward silence, which was strange since lately when he and I talked, everything was always so smooth. He opened the door to his car and I could tell he was excited about something, and he clearly wanted to say something, but he wasn't sure how to do it. Much to my delight, however, he finally mustered the courage and just did it.

"There's something I wanted to ask you. It's a little unusual and I completely understand if you say no, but well, since we've been going out for a few weeks now and since I've been formally introduced to your family, I was wondering if you would consider wearing this. And I know it's not a Monroe jacket; since I'm new here and I don't have one yet, but it's my jacket from last year in Huckstin so I thought you might like it anyway."

He reached into the car and pulled out a letterman's jacket. It was maroon and navy, with a huge H on the front, Logan's last name on the back, and numerous badges on the left sleeve.

He held it up for me to see. "I think it would look good on you. Maroon is nice with your hair."

I snatched it from him so fast I didn't even know what I had done. I don't know why he had been so nervous; not only would I wear it, I'd probably never take it off. I wasted no time slipping it on. It was bulky and way too big for me, especially through the shoulders and around the waist, but I didn't care, not one single bit.

I had a letterman's jacket.

Logan's letterman's jacket.

I was the happiest girl in the world.

October 10

I was the talk of school all week. The minute I showed up on Monday morning, everyone saw what I was wearing and their eyes got big. I tried to act nonchalant, like a lot of women do after they receive an engagement ring, but to be honest I couldn't wait for people to mention it. Most people were really excited and positive and they showered me with compliments, but I could tell some of them, including Hailey Wetmore, weren't. They were jealous. They wanted to be the girlfriend of the school's star running back.

Too bad for them.

I didn't mind the fact it wasn't a Monroe jacket at all. If anything, I liked it. It made me unique. The other girls had black and orange jackets that were awesome, but they pretty much all looked the same. Mine, by contrast, was completely different. It was maroon and navy, and Logan was right. It went perfectly with my hair and I should know since I spent over an hour the night before standing in front of the mirror admiring it.

The attention regarding my new jacket was great, but the highlight of the week happened on Friday. I went to the football game and guess who showed up? My dad. He came over and stood next to me in the bleachers.

"What are you doing here, dad? I never expected to see you at a game."

"I kept thinking about what Logan said. He's right. I've been away from these games far too long. I need to see another game, if nothing else just for old time's sake."

The game started minutes later and we cheered as Monroe took the field, with Caleb and Logan at the front of the squad, as usual. We booed as Arlington came out. There was the national anthem, the coin toss, and the kickoff, and Arlington got the ball first, but I didn't really care about that and don't tell anyone but I really only watch when Logan is on the field. As soon as we got the ball, I got excited and turned to my dad.

"Get ready. It's showtime."

And indeed it was. On the first play, Caleb made a nice pass to one of the receivers, then did a handoff to the fullback on the next. But the real fireworks didn't begin until the third play.

Caleb handed the ball to Logan. Logan rumbled eight yards and it took three defenders to take him down.

My dad nodded. "Not bad. Not bad at all."

The next few plays were more of the same. Logan went around the left side of the line for a five-yard gain, then on the next play rushed for five more. But then something truly amazing happened. Caleb pitched the ball to Logan and Logan ran with it to the right side of the field.

"Sweep right," my dad said as he watched. But then his eyes got big. "There's nothing there, Logan. Cut back against the grain."

The line of blockers in front of Logan collapsed, with bodies flying everywhere, and there was nowhere for him to go. So he slammed on the brakes and did exactly what my dad had said. He cut back to the left and raced into the middle of the field. A defender moved to intercept him.

"Pick up the receiver's block," my dad said.

Logan angled to the left, just enough to get behind one of his teammates, who knocked the incoming defender to the side. And then it was nothing but a sprint. Sixty yards later, Logan was standing in the end zone celebrating. Our bleachers went crazy and the band played an especially lively version of *Tequila*.

My dad was nothing but smiles. "That's how you do it, Angel. Did you see how Logan felt out his blockers and how he was aware of his surroundings, even when the play didn't develop as designed? That's great field recognition. Great awareness. And great improvisation on his part. You can't teach that kind of stuff. That's natural talent. Go Bearcats!"

To be honest, I didn't really have a clue what he was talking about and I had absolutely no idea what field recognition and awareness was, but I didn't care. As long as he was happy with Logan, I was happy.

And boy was he happy. Logan scored two more touchdowns and we won the game easily, beating Arlington 28-3. The three of us celebrated afterward by going to a nearby mall and my dad treated us to ice cream and other goodies.

October 14

Today was the first day of my team's big 'out-of-state' trip for the fall season, and it was in Las Vegas. I was actually a little sad because I knew I wouldn't be able to see Logan for three days, which seemed like an eternity to me, but he made me feel a little better just before we left for the airport.

"Don't worry. I'll send you texts and throw in some goofy selfies to keep your spirits up while you're gone. Sound okay?"

"I guess so," I said, but really it didn't. I didn't want to be away from him even for a minute.

"But it's on one condition."

I raised an eyebrow.

"Have you ever hit a home run in Vegas before?"

I shook my head. This was my first trip to Las Vegas so I'd never gotten any hits, of any type, there, let alone something as big as a home run.

"Then you need to hit a home run for me."

Instantly I grew apprehensive. "I don't hit too many home runs. It's pretty tough."

"You can do it. That's how you got Homer, right?"

I was about to say something in response when he interrupted.

"Have faith. And send word as soon as it happens. I know it will."

So off to Vegas I went. And unfortunately, getting there turned out to be quite a chore. Lea's parents didn't come so she flew with my dad, Homer, and me. Homer had to ride in a doggy carryon cage, which had had plenty of room for him but he didn't like it anyway. We had a layover in Oakland. Oakland is a small airport, but a nice one, and we had dinner at California Pizza Kitchen, but just as we finished dinner there was announcement our flight was delayed for two hours. So Lea and I killed the time playing cards, with Homer in his carryon case, and he's a lot heavier than I originally realized. I was really sweating as we trudged our way back to our gate for boarding. Finally, our plane was ready and we departed, but it was already 10:00 pm by the time we got to Las Vegas. We were pretty tired, and then we had to stand in a line for a rental car for almost forty-five minutes. And it was pretty ridiculous since we were the next people in line but it still took what seemed like forever to get a car. Rental car companies need to make some serious improvements when it comes to customer service. Anyway, we finally got a car, but then it was another thirty minutes until we got to our hotel in a suburb in northern Las Vegas. I was getting pretty cranky by then since I tend to do that when I get tired, but my attitude changed completely when I saw our hotel.

It wasn't a hotel, at least not the way I picture them. It was the hotel of my dreams. It was huge, with multiple wings, and in many ways it resembled a resort more than a hotel. My dad went to check us in at the front desk, and Lea, Homer, and I darted around, taking a look at everything we could. There was a small mall in the lobby, with numerous shops, a huge fitness/workout center, with a million treadmills, and a pool with a gorgeous waterfall. I thought I had died and gone to heaven. A few minutes before, I had been nodding off in the car. Now, I was wide awake and full of energy. I wanted to get my swimming suit and jump in the pool at that very moment. But it was way too late for that so we headed up to our room and my mouth fell open the minute I opened the door and looked inside. It was huge, with two of the biggest beds I have ever seen, a walk-in wardrobe/closet, and a bathroom that was bigger than my bedroom at home.

"We need to play tournaments in Vegas more often," I said.

"You can say that again," Lea said.

October 15

Unfortunately, the excitement of arriving in Las Vegas was dampened this morning when the drama began. My team is a great team and I really like it but there is one thing I always hate.

Picking our uniforms for the day. It's always an excruciating ordeal and today was no exception. It all began when Laura sent a text message to the rest of us saying we should wear black pants, jerseys, and socks. But then Casey responded by saying, "Are you crazy? We're in Vegas. It's gonna be 100° today. We'll die in solid black. Let's wear gray jerseys, pants, and socks." But then I responded by saying, "I hate solid gray. It's so blah. Let's wear gray jerseys, black pants, and gray socks." But then Olivia responded, "OMG. You can't wear gray socks with black pants. That's so 90s. Let's wear gray jerseys, black pants, and black socks." And then Kristin responded, "I wouldn't be caught dead in that combo. Let's go for black jerseys, gray pants, and gray socks."

Not knowing what else to do, I got out my uniform, spread it out on the bed in front of us, and arranged it to match Kristin's proposed combo, which sounded okay to me, and what do you know? It did look good. So I texted back to her, "Sounds good to me." So Lea and I got dressed and did our hair, because you can't play softball unless your hair looks good, then we went down to the lobby to meet the other girls for breakfast, but when we got down there we saw the other girls were wearing Kristin's uniform combo with one exception: they were wearing one gray sock and one black sock.

Kristin looked at us and shook her head. "Didn't you get the last text? We decided to mix up the socks a bit."

Lea and I sighed, then trudged back upstairs to change our socks so we matched everyone else.

My dad shook his head. "Why can't you girls be like boys? Boys don't care about their uniforms. They'll wear whatever uniform they find lying on the floor. And it doesn't even have to be clean."

"That's gross," I said, and we headed back downstairs for breakfast.

Despite the uniform fiasco, the day went well. It was really hot, almost 100° by noon, but we had fun anyway. Our first game was against a team from Reno called the Gold Rush. We won 3-2. I got one hit, a single that scored Hannah and Casey. Our second game was against a team from California called the Bat Busters and they killed us. I'd like to list the highlights but there were none. But we made up for it in the day's finale, beating a team from Arizona 5-4. I got a single and a double but Kristin was the real hero. She won the game by hitting a massive home run in the bottom half of the final inning.

And then I remembered something. I had promised Logan I would hit a home run for him. But so far, I hadn't even come close. We went back to the hotel, played in the pool for an hour, then went to the Strip for a stroll. The dads and coaches went to a restaurant for a steak dinner, which is a tradition of theirs, and we girls roamed up and down the street, admiring the shops and looking for something fun to do. I had never been to Las Vegas before so I was pretty amazed. The neon lights were super bright and the place was so busy and lively. We went on a roller coaster at a casino, then grabbed dinner at Subway, which I thought was funny because of all of the restaurants in Las Vegas, many of which were very fancy, we chose Subway. It was good nonetheless. I ordered my favorite, a 6" sweet onion chicken teriyaki on wheat bread with extra olives. After that we headed back to the hotel. I didn't like the idea of leaving Homer in the hotel room for too long by himself. He's still pretty young and he gets lonely pretty quickly. And I didn't want to risk any 'accidents' on the carpet.

Right before I went to bed, I got a text from Logan. "Any luck with my home run?"

"Not yet."

"You'll get it soon. I know you will."

I hoped he was right. Like always, I didn't want to disappoint him.

October 16

I can't believe it but Logan was right. Our first game today was against a team from northern Nevada called the Lone Wolves. They had cool uniforms with fancy stripes but their name seemed strange and highly contradictory to me. How can you be lone, and yet be wolves? Shouldn't it be Lone Wolf? Anyway, the Lone Wolves were leading 3-1 when I got my second at-bat in the bottom of the fifth inning. I had popped out during my first at-bat. We had two runners, Haley and Casey, on base and two outs. The Lone Wolves' pitcher was a tall, thin girl with straight, blonde hair and she threw really hard, but she didn't have great control of her pitches and sometimes left them over the middle of the plate. I waited patiently for the right pitch, then swung with everything I had.

This one's for Logan, I thought. And then I hit it.

And I didn't just hit it. I killed it. I knew it was a home run the minute it left my bat. It went even further than the first home run I had hit, the one that had won me Homer. Everyone cheered as I rounded the bases and stepped on home plate. My dad patted me on the back and Homer licked my face. But the best compliment of all came from afar.

"I knew you could do it," Logan texted. "Pitchers beg for mercy when they see you step up to the plate."

I smiled. He was a good boyfriend. I will need to keep him for a while.

We had two more games later that day and we won one of them. I got two hits, a pair of doubles, in the first game and one hit, a triple, in the second. All-in-all, it was a fun day and I hope we get to return to Nevada for another tournament in the not-so-distant future, but for now, I can't wait to get home and see Logan again.

October 23

Logan had a game today and it was a big one because it was the first round of the state's playoff tournament. My dad came and he was really excited.

"The playoffs are always a big deal. It'll be great if they win. When I played at Monroe we won the league championship every year but we never won a playoff game. One game was close but the others were blowouts. So if they win today Logan will have done something I never managed to do."

"Do you think they have a chance? I heard this other team is really good. People at school are saying they have a nosebacker who is so good he can win games by himself."

My dad chuckled. "He's a nose tackle, Angel. I read about him in the paper. His name is Reggie James. He's good, there's no doubt about that, but I'm still not sure he's a match for Logan. Logan is outstanding."

The game started minutes later and it was a spectacular battle. I was so nervous I could barely hold still. I started shewing on my nails, which is something I haven't done for years. The other team was a school from Tacoma called Stadium and they were impressive. Every player was huge, and most of them were lightning fast. They knew Logan was one of our best players, if not our best, so everywhere he went, they followed, with Reggie James usually leading the way. They swarmed him every time he got the ball and the strategy was largely effective, but Logan never gave up and on a handoff in the third quarter he finally broke free, into the clear, and rambled twenty yards to Stadium's three-yard line. It took three defenders to take him down. On the next play, he went straight through the middle and punched it in for the touchdown. Reggie James grabbed him by an arm but was unable to stop him.

That was all we needed. The final score was 7-0.

October 25

I saw one of the dumbest things today. We had a game against a team from Bellevue called the Beast, and all of their players got really excited when their starting pitcher showed up. Their dugout was a flurry of activity as she arrived and she had something in her arms. It was wrapped in blankets and she put it on the bench.

"What is it?" I asked Lea. She sat to my right, watching all of the commotion with me.

"They heard how popular Homer is so they got a mascot of their own. He's making his debut today. His name is Beast."

I looked over and saw a tiny dog sitting on the bench. I didn't know exactly what type of dog it was, and I didn't really care, but it was one of those designer dogs rich women carry around in their purses. It was so small my cat, Cinnamon, could have eaten it for breakfast.

"That's a mascot?" Kristin asked.

"Its name is Beast?" Olivia asked.

"That's ridiculous," Casey said.

And it was. Beast didn't do anything the whole game. He just sat there, shivering in the cold. Unlike Homer, he didn't lead his team during their warm-up exercises, he didn't bark when his players made good plays, and he didn't chase after foul balls for Blue.

Speaking of Blue, we had the same one who umpired the first game I brought Homer too, the same one who was so amazed and thankful Homer retrieved foul balls for him. He looked at Beast and shook his head in disgust.

"That's no Homer," he said.

"You can say that again," I said.

October 27

Today was a strange day. It started off really poorly. Chloe got in a fight with my dad. She's seventeen and she wants a car but my dad doesn't want to get her one. It's been an issue since the day Chloe got her driver's license and it boils over on occasion, including today.

"It's not like cars are that expensive."

My dad raised an eyebrow. "Not that expensive? Have you looked at car prices lately?"

"I just did, online. There's a great VW Jetta at a dealership in the U district. It's only $18,000."

My dad scoffed. "Only $18,000? Where are you going to get $18,000? Do you think $18,000 grows on trees?"

"Don't you have some money saved up? I thought most people saved money."

"Some people save money. And yes, I have some money saved up. But it's not for something silly like a car. It's for something important."

"Like what?"

"Like an emergency. Or your college tuition."

"I don't need any money for college. I'm going to get a softball scholarship."

"That's great if you do but we can't count on it, Chloe. Scholarships are hard to get and you just never know. You may get turned down, or hurt, or whatever. I want to have money just in case."

Chloe stomped her foot on the ground. "If I don't get a scholarship I'm not going."

"What do you mean?"

"If a college doesn't give me a scholarship, then screw them. I'm not going. They're not worth my time."

"That's a terrible attitude. Don't ever say things like that. That kind of attitude will get you nowhere in life."

"I don't care. I want a car. And think about how nice it would be for everyone, dad, including you. You wouldn't have to drive me around all the time."

"I don't mind driving you around, Chloe. That's my job. That's what parents do."

Chloe sighed. She turned to me and gave me a look as though she wanted me to help her out. I was sitting on the couch, just a few feet away, but there was no way I was getting involved in this one. Homer sat next to me. He had his head on the couch and a sad look on his face. He didn't want to get involved in this argument either and he hated it when there was conflict among family members.

When she saw I wasn't going to assist her in any way, she continued the discussion herself. And she was clearly getting desperate. "I'll find a cheap one, a used one. Something, anything, please dad."

My dad sighed. "I just don't think it's a good idea. You haven't been driving for that long and you're not that experienced. You need more time before you get a car of your own. I don't want any accidents or speeding tickets."

"I'm a good driver. You said so yourself, just the other day, remember?"

"You're an excellent driver when I'm with you. But I'm not sure how you'll do on your own. You're going to be racing all over town with your friends in the car, not paying attention, and you'll probably be texting while you're doing it."

"No way. I'd never do that."

My dad stared straight at her. "You're a teenage girl. Your phone is glued to your hand. What's the longest you've ever gone without sending a text?"

Chloe looked offended. "That's ridiculous. I can't believe you just said that. I don't text that often."

"Yes, you do. And look, you've got a text right now."

Reflexively, Chloe turned and grabbed her phone. But then she saw my dad had fooled her. There was no message.

"That's not funny, dad. Stop messing with me. All of my friends have cars. It's embarrassing to be the only one without one. I feel like an outcast. A pariah."

"I'm not getting you a car to enhance your social standing, Chloe. That's ridiculous. That's the worst reason yet."

"Amy's dad got her a car and she barely had to ask for it. And it's super nice. It's a Mustang."

Chloe was talking about one of her teammates on the Wildcats, a girl named Amy Ferguson. She's their catcher. Her dad had bought her a Ford Mustang. It was a used one, but it had low mileage for its age and was in great shape. I saw it at school a couple of weeks ago and was immediately impressed. It's gray with black trim and matching wheels.

My dad nodded. "I spoke to Amy's dad about that. Amy earned it."

"What?"

"Her dad said he wasn't going to get it for her, but she's been working so hard he couldn't resist."

"What do you mean?"

"He said she's been practicing at least two hours every day for the past two months and he doesn't even have to ask her anymore. She just goes out and does it. And she's been doing really well as a result. Her batting average is over .400 this season."

I couldn't help but agree. The last time I watched one of Chloe's games, Amy was spectacular. She got two singles, a double, and made a stellar play on defense.

Chloe sighed. "Whatever. She's still not as good as me."

"I don't care if she's as good as you or not. All I care about is how hard you've been working. Amy's been working really hard so she earned her car. How hard have you been working lately?"

Chloe didn't say anything.

"How many times have you practiced this week, other than your official team practices?"

Chloe didn't say anything and she didn't need to. We all knew the answer. On her own, she hadn't practiced at all this week, or last week, or the week before that.

"So I don't know why we're even having this conversation," my dad said. "You're old enough to know how the world works. If you want something from someone, you need to do what they want. And I want you to practice more. So don't ask me about a car again until I see some serious effort on your part. You say you're going to win a scholarship but I don't see much work being done to get it. As such, I wouldn't get your hopes up."

Chloe was so offended she stomped out of the room as quickly and as loudly as she could. I could hear her footsteps all the way up the stairs.

My dad turned to me. "Don't you ever act like that. If you do, you're grounded for a week."

I sighed. I hated it when he did that. I hadn't done anything, I was just sitting there minding my own business, but I got a reprimand anyway. Guilt by association, I guess.

A few minutes later, Chloe was back, with a big frown on her face. She tossed my mitt into my lap.

"Come on. Apparently, I need to practice and I can't do it without a catcher."

"I'm busy." Really, I wasn't, I was just playing *Tetris* on my phone, but I felt like being lazy for a while.

My dad intervened. "Get moving, Angel. You could use the practice, too."

And then he turned to Homer. "And you go with them and make certain they work hard. I don't want to hear they were taking water breaks every five minutes."

I wasn't too happy about it but I didn't have a choice, so we rounded up our gear, went to McCall Park, and worked on Chloe's pitching. I wore my old catcher's gear and backstopped for her. I could tell she was really annoyed because she throws really hard when she's upset, even harder than normal, and in no time my hand was stinging. I had to take a small break to let it recover. I shook it out, then had Homer lick it to make it feel better.

Chloe saw my hand and apologized. "Sorry. Dad just makes me so upset sometimes. He doesn't understand. Wait 'til you turn sixteen and want a car. Then you'll know what I'm going through."

She was about to say something more when a car pulled up. It was Caleb and Logan.

Apparently, they had been driving by and saw us so they stopped to say hi.

"What are you two doing out here?" Caleb asked Chloe.

"What's it look like? Apparently, if I practice for two hours every day for the next two months, I might get a car. But I'm not getting my hopes up, not with my dad."

Caleb and Logan nodded. They didn't really know what Chloe was talking about, but they both knew the best way to deal with a high-maintenance girl like her was to just nod and play along. Especially when she was in a foul mood.

"Mind if we join in?" Caleb asked. "I want to bat."

"That's stupid," Chloe said. "You can't bat."

He chcukled. "I'm the star quarterback for the varsity football team, Chloe. I can do anything if I put my mind to it."

"Really? Is that so? Just because you're good at football means you're good at everything?"

"Not everything. But I think I can hit a stupid ball. Especially a softball. It's a girl's game after all."

I cringed the minute he said it. Chloe was already in a bad mood, and making a sexist comment like that in front of her was a big mistake.

"A girl's game?"

She had one hand on her hip and an eyebrow raised as she said it. I've seen that look before. Trust me, nothing good happens when Chloe gives you that look.

He saw her posture and tried quickly to right his wrong. "Not that there's anything wrong with that. Girls sports are great. But come on. If you girls can do it, then we football players can. Throw me a pitch. I'll show you."

Chloe chuckled. "Okay, but don't start crying when you get hurt." She took her spot in the pitching circle and Caleb grabbed a bat from her softball bag. Somewhat hesitantly, I took my place behind the plate. Logan and Homer sat in the bleachers. Homer wouldn't watch. He knew this was going to get ugly and he didn't want to see it when it did.

The first pitch was so fast Caleb didn't even react. He just stood there as the ball exploded in my mitt.

Chloe looked at him. "You just gonna stand there all day? You can't hit the ball unless you take that bat off your shoulder."

Caleb had a stupid look on his face and no response whatsoever. He had had no idea the pitch was going to be that fast.

The next pitch was just as nasty. This time, he actually managed to swing at it but his reaction was way too late. Chloe laughed at him.

"What's wrong? I thought football players could do anything. Especially this. This is just a girl's game, right?"

Caleb got really serious. He was a star athlete, one of the best at our school, and he was determined to prove it to Chloe.

But Chloe fooled him completely. She threw a changeup and it was a dandy. It was at least twenty miles per hour slower than her previous pitch. Caleb was so caught off guard he couldn't adjust in time. He had already completed his swing and had the bat on his opposite shoulder by the time the pitch got to the plate.

Logan fell over in the stands laughing. He had never seen anything so funny.

Caleb turned to him and he was clearly irritated by his response. He wasn't used to being embarrassed, especially by a girl. "You think you can do any better? Get up here and try it."

Logan shook his head. "No way. I know better. These softball girls are the real deal. We had this one girl back at my school in Huckstin. One day, the baseball players were making fun of her so she had them line up and she pitched to them and struck them out. Every one of them, in order, without even breaking a sweat. It was the craziest thing I've ever seen. They never made fun of her again and some of them started asking her for tips."

It took a minute but Caleb finally softened, then handed the bat back to Chloe. "Maybe you're right. Maybe we football players should stick with football and let you softball players take care of softball."

"That's a good idea," Chloe said. "And it's a good thing you learned your lesson when you did."

Caleb raised an eyebrow. "Why?"

"Because the next pitch was going to be a brushback."

"What's a brushback?"

I couldn't help but intervene. "You don't want to know."

October 30

Today was the second round of the state football playoffs but it didn't go well. Our game was against a school called Jackson and they were the defending champions. I knew we were in trouble right from the start. They were huge. Every one of them was over six feet tall and many of them were over 250 pounds. They made Logan, Caleb, and the rest of our team look small by comparison. They hadn't lost a game all year and most of them had been blowouts.

The most noteworthy thing about them, however, was their kicker. It was a girl. I was in complete shock when she ran onto the field and began her warmups. Her name was Kiana Cruise and she was tall and lean, with dark hair that hung from the back of her helmet. My dad wasted little time giving me the details.

"I saw a couple of articles about her last year. As you can probably guess, she was quite a sensation, especially at first. Jackson's normal kicker got hurt so they were desperate and they gave her a tryout. She did great and even ended up scoring a touchdown in one game."

I raised an eyebrow. "I didn't know kickers scored touchdowns."

"Normally, they don't, but it was a trick play. Jackson line up to kick a field goal but snapped the ball straight to Kiana. She grabbed it and took it to the endzone. I wish I could have seen it."

I was fascinated and was going to ask some more about her but never got the chance. The game began and it was a battle from the start. Every play was epic and the hits were huge. Jackson jumped to a quick lead, 14-0, but we battled back and tied it by halftime. Logan scored a touchdown on a sweep and Caleb scored a touchdown on a quarterback keeper. In the fourth quarter, we kicked a field goal to take the lead, but Jackson came back with a field goal of their own, and then another, and another. Kiana kicked all three of them and she made them easily, including a long one from around midfield. As such, Jackson led 23-17 with thirty seconds to play. After a timeout, we marched down the field and Logan made one final, gallant dive toward the endzone to win it for us, but the defenders swarmed him and knocked him to the ground. The final whistle sounded as he was lying there, with the ball in his hands, at the one-yard line.

Normally after games, Logan meets me briefly along the sideline before he goes to the locker room to shower and change. It gives him a chance to say hi and it gives me a chance to compliment him on his performance. But today he didn't. Instead, I found him sitting on the players' bench at the far side of the field with one of the assistant coaches at his side.

"You're a great player, Logan. Keep your chin up. We'll get them next year."

I waited until the coach had walked away, then sat down next to Logan on the bench. The minute I saw his face, I became concerned. I saw something I had never seen before.

He had tears in his eyes.

At first, I didn't know what to do. I knew football meant a lot to him but I didn't know it meant this much.

"Are you okay?"

"I can't believe it. One yard. One stupid yard. That's all I needed."

His helmet was lying on the ground near his feet. He kicked it to the side.

"You did your best."

"I wanted to win."

"We all did, but ultimately it's just a game."

"I know. But winning means a lot to this school. And this school has been really good to me ever since I got here. You've all treated me so well. I wanted to give you something — a state title — in return."

"You don't owe us anything, Logan. And even if you did, look what you did give us. Last week, you gave us a playoff victory. My dad said Monroe had never won a playoff game before you came along. Even back when he played. So you gave us that. And that was a big deal to him and he's pretty hard to impress. Trust me, I know."

"A state title would have been better."

"True, but like your coach said, there's always next year."

"Not for me. I won't be here, remember? I have to return to Texas."

I paused. I had forgotten about that and for good reason. It was something I didn't like to think about. I didn't like the thought of Logan leaving, not one bit. But I needed to worry about that another day. Today, I needed to make Logan feel better and realize what he had accomplished.

"You guys did great this year and it was quite a ride. I don't even like football very much but I had a good time. This was the only game you lost all year, and to Jackson. They're the defending champions for a reason. Those guys are huge."

It took a minute but finally he smiled. "You can say that again. Especially that inside linebacker, Murphy. Wow. I haven't seen a kid like that in a long time. It's funny. They always say everything is so big in Texas, including the football players, but you've got some big players here in Washington, too, especially on that team. What do they feed them?"

"Venti white chocolate mochas with a shot of steroids, two on game days, with whipped cream on top, of course. You've got to have whipped cream with your steroids."

My comment was completely ridiculous and I couldn't believe I said it but apparently it worked. Logan couldn't help but smile. And then he asked me a question.

"Did you see their kicker? It was a girl. Is it common in Washington to have girls on football teams?"

I responded immediately. "No, not at all. That girl, Kiana, is a special case."

"I was impressed. She was really good. Cute, too."

I raised an eyebrow the minute he said it so he wasted no time elaborating. "In a subjective way, you know. She's not as cute as you of course."

I couldn't help but chuckle. I didn't really like him making comments about how cute other girls were but I'm not the jealous type and all I really wanted at that particular point in time was to make him feel better.

"How are you feeling now?"

He shrugged but didn't say anything. He looked a little better but not too much.

"Maybe this will help," I said.

I leaned forward and kissed him.

To be one hundred percent honest, I still can't believe I did it. Normally, I wasn't that aggressive and I had never kissed a boy before, but it just seemed like the right thing to do.

"How do you feel now?"

His eyes were big. It was obvious I had caught him by surprise.

"A little better."

"Just a little? Then maybe you need another."

I kissed him again. By the time our second kiss was completed, his mood had changed and he had pretty much forgotten about football entirely.

"Some of the guys are going out to dinner tonight. I guess it's an end-of-the-season tradition or something. Do you want to go with me?"

"Of course. It sounds like fun."

We hopped up, and, hand-in-hand, walked off of the field.

November 25

Thanksgiving Day. I'm so stuffed I'm going to die. My mom made garlic mashed potatoes and I love them so I had three servings. Even Homer and Cinnamon are stuffed. They got special dinners, too. I don't usually let them have 'people' food but since it's a holiday I thought I'd make an exception. I gave them a little bit of everything and they gobbled it up happily. Cinnamon even ate his carrots which surprised me because I didn't think cats liked vegetables.

December 10

Today was a grand and glorious day. It snowed last night, at least six inches, so they cancelled school. And thank goodness since I didn't do my homework last night. I meant to but I got too busy watching *The Cake Boss* and by the time it was over I was too tired. Anyway, since it only snows once or twice a year in the Pacific Northwest it's a big deal when it does, so Chloe and I slipped on our boots, jackets, and gloves and headed outside to frolic in it for a few minutes. And it was really fun since it was Homer's first time in the snow. At first, he didn't know what to do. It was pretty deep, up to his belly, so he just stood on the patio and looked at me like, "You gotta be kidding me." But as soon as Chloe and I darted out into it and started goofing around he followed because he never likes to be left behind. We made snow angels, built a snowman, and started a snowball fight, but it quickly evolved into just Chloe and me throwing snowballs at Homer, and he loved every minute of it. He didn't actually catch any, they just exploded in his mouth, but he loved it anyway. After about half an hour, however, he stopped playing and disappeared for a few seconds.

"Where'd Homer go?" I asked.

"Don't know," Chloe said.

It didn't take us long to figure out what had happened. When we walked over to the side of the house, near my dad's tool shed, what did we see?

Yellow snow.

December 25

It's Christmas Day and, like most Christmas Days, it was great fun. Everyone got a load of loot, including Homer. He got three new chew toys, one of which he tore up immediately, plus a tug-of-war rope and a fancy new serving dish. It was one of those elevated ones that are good for a dog's back because they don't have to bend down to eat their food. Dogs have it good nowadays. Cinnamon got some goodies, too, including a new collar and a toy that was filled with catnip. He was as high as a kite in no time. In the meantime, I got a bunch of things. My mom got me some new jeans because my old ones were getting pretty tight and I don't care what the scale in the bathroom says I have not gained five pounds. I decided to go easy on dinner anyway, just to be safe. But I did have an extra serving of my mom's garlic mashed potatoes because they're evil and cannot be resisted. Chloe got me a purse, a really cute one that came with a matching wallet. She's so good at picking things like that. My dad got me a new bat, this year's version of the Stealth, because it's supposed to be the hottest bat on the market.

"With that bat you'll tear it up, Angel. I hear it has some serious pop."

It was all great but the best present I got, by far, was from Logan. It was a necklace with a heart-shaped pendant hanging from it, and when you opened the pendant it had a photo inside. And the photo was the best one he could have picked. I don't remember who took it, or when, or where, but it had me on the right, Logan on the left with his arm around me, and Homer in the middle. Like always, Homer's tongue was hanging out the side of his mouth.

Chloe took a look at it and even she was impressed.

"You know, as far as boyfriends go, that Logan's not bad. Not bad at all."

I stood in front of the mirror, in the bathroom, staring at my new necklace for the remainder of the night.

January 15

I don't know how she did it, maybe she just wore him down, but Chloe finally pulled it off. She talked my dad into getting her a car. They went shopping and came home with it a few hours later. And it was really cute. It was a silver Volkswagen Jetta. It was a few years old but was in great shape, with low mileage and no dents or scrapes or anything. Chloe was as happy as a clam. She took a selfie of herself in front of it and texted it to all of her friends. She took Homer and me out for a drive so she could show it off to us. We stopped at Cold Stone Creamery on the way home and got goodies. Chloe and I, like most sisters, have a strange relationship. Some days we get along fine and other days we fight like cats and dogs, especially on days when she stays in the bathroom all morning doing her makeup and I have to wait for my turn. I've called her a few bad names on days like that. Today, however, we got along great and I enjoyed every minute of our time together.

And it's good news for me, too. Next year, when I get my driver's license, I'm going to want a car, too. And now that my dad got one for Chloe he'll have no choice but to get one for me, too. That would only be fair, right? Well done, Chloe.

February 14

Today was Valentine's Day and it was the best Valentine's Day ever. Logan took me to dinner, to a fancy, Italian restaurant in downtown Seattle, and it was really exciting because we dressed up. Logan looks stunning in a suit, especially the one he wore, which was dark gray with pinstripes. His tie was navy blue and it went perfectly with his suit. I wore a tight, red dress Chloe helped me pick out at the mall last week. My dad wasn't too happy about it and said it showed way too much skin, but luckily he let me wear it anywat. Logan liked it and said it was hot. He gave me a dozen white roses, a box of chocolates, and a teddy bear he made at that store in the mall where you can make your own stuffed animals. He dressed it in a softball uniform and it even had a miniature bat and ball. And tiny cleats on its feet. It was absolutely adorable.

Dinner was spectacular. I ordered lasagna and it was delicious. Logan got seafood fettuccine and he let me have a few bites to see how it was. It was as good as my lasagna, if not better. After dinner, we went to a movie, then he dropped me off at home. Normally, Chloe and I have a 10:00 pm curfew but my dad extended it to midnight since it was Valentine's Day. Chloe was waiting for me at the door. She, too, had gone out for dinner, with Caleb, and she had arrived home just a few minutes before I did.

She had a smile on her face. "What'd you think of the softball bear?"

My eyes got big. "You knew about that?"

"Logan showed it to me the other day at school. It's so cute. He said it took him an hour to pick out the jersey. He got the gray one because it was the one that looked the most like your Sky jersey."

I was nothing but smiles the rest of the night. I took my softball bear upstairs and set it on my bed, right in the middle of my pillows. Homer's eyes got big the minute he saw it. He likes to chew on things, including my white sandals which I'm still upset about, and to him my softball bear was nothing more than another thing to sink his teeth into.

"Don't even think about it."

He hopped off the bed and, with a dejected look on his face, headed down the hall.

March 16

Logan is the best boyfriend ever. I don't know how he did it but before school this morning, when I wasn't looking, he slipped notes into my belongings. I found the first one a couple of hours later when I was in math class and my teacher, Mr. McEnroe, told us to open our books to page 127. The minute I grabbed my book I saw something sticking out of the top of it and I thought it was a bookmark of some sort. Upon closer examination, however, I saw it was a small note, not much bigger than a business card, in a miniature envelope. Later, Logan confessed to me he had made the envelopes himself and it had taken him over two hours to do it. The note read, "I miss you." Of course that brought a smile to my lips. But it didn't end there and, incredibly, got better. An hour later, in history class, I opened my history book and there was another note. This one read, "I miss you really bad." An hour later, in English class, I opened my book and found another note. This one read, "Do you miss me?" At that point, I started wondering how many notes he had hidden and I tore through the rest of my books as fast as I could. Ms. Ferguson, my English teacher, shot me a curious glance as she saw me sitting at my desk, digging frantically through my belongings, and she probably thought

I had gone crazy. Anyway, I found three more notes, including one in the front pocket of my backpack. They all had cute messages on them and each was sillier than its predecessor. One of them was a drawing of three stick figures. The tallest stick figure wore a football helmet, the second stick figure wore a softball mitt, and the third stick figure was a dog. I showed all of my notes, including the drawing of the stick figures, to Lea.

"You're the luckiest girl in the world. Why can't I have a boyfriend like that?"

So I decided I needed to do something for him. As soon as school ended for the day, I went to the bookstore and got some fancy paper, the type usually used for making certificates, and a package of foil seals and I made him a 'Boyfriend of the Year' award. I designed it on my computer and printed it on my dad's laser printer, and with the fancy paper and the foil seal it looked really official. A couple of hours later, I met him for dessert at Starbucks and gave it to him and his eyes lit up the minute he saw it. We both laughed. What a great day. It's amazing how even the smallest thing, like a note or two from your boyfriend, can turn a normal day into an extraordinary one.

May 15

I'm going to shoot myself. Today, my team had a tournament in Kent, a city about fifteen miles southeast of Seattle. Unlike most tournaments which last the whole weekend, this one was only for a day, and it started well. Our first game was against a Canadian team called the Leafs. Like most Canadian teams, they were really good but we jumped to a quick lead and held on to win 4-3. Our second game was against the Redmond LadyCats and we cruised to an easy victory, winning 10-1. I used my new bat, the one my dad got me for Christmas, and I got two hits in the first game and three in the second.

But that was the end of my fun. Our final game was against my old team, the Eastside Angels, and my archrival, Ashley Martinez. It was the first time I had faced her since the game back in the fall when she completely embarrassed me. I'm still recovering from that one. As such, I was really determined to do well and I really wanted to get back at her. But things didn't start well. Ashley's first pitch was a riseball and I hit the bottom of it and launched it a mile — straight up. The Angels' catcher caught it for an easy out.

"Can't get 'em all," Ashley said in her typical, arrogant way.

My next at-bat came in the fourth inning and it didn't go any better. Ashley got two quick strikes on me and finished me off with a fastball. I hit it, but weakly, and it went straight to the second baseman. I was out by a mile.

My final at-bat came in the sixth inning. I dug my cleats into the dirt and tapped my bat on the plate, and I was really determined to get a hit this time. But once again, my hopes were short lived. I hit the first pitch straight at the first baseman. She didn't even have to move to make the catch.

"Softball isn't easy," Ashley said as I trudged back to the dugout.

It's official. I hate her. If it's the last thing I do, I'm going to get her, and I'm going to get her good.

May 22

I'm starting to get worried. It's less than a month until Logan has to move back to Texas. I may never see him again. And even if I do, I won't get to see him very often, at most once or twice a year, and even that much may be a long shot. I don't know what I'm going to do. My eyes get glossy whenever I think about it. This year has been so wonderful, first when I got Homer, and then when I met Logan, I never want it to end.

Logan and I sat at Starbucks talking about it.

"There's no way you can stay for another year? You said you liked it here."

Logan responded immediately. "This place is awesome. I love it here. But I already asked my uncle, a couple of times. He's been really generous but he can't afford to support me for another year. And it doesn't matter anyway; even if he could, my dad wouldn't allow it. My dad didn't want me to come here in the first place, remember? It was my idea. I was the one who insisted. And there's no way I can convince him to let me stay for another year. Trust me, I already tried."

"What about the summer? At least you could stay until the end of summer."

Logan shook his head. "My mom gets custody of me during the summer. And my dad says if I don't go, he'll be in contempt of court and he'll get in trouble with the judge. Something to do with a parenting plan or a residential schedule or something. I don't really know what that means but I don't want to get him in any trouble especially with the law. He has enough to worry about with my stepmother and my younger brothers."

So that was that. Like it or not, Logan was moving back to Texas on the last day of the school year. As such, I better enjoy these final few weeks. They're all I've got.

June 1

Homer is a hero. He saved us all. Well, four of us. It all started on Friday afternoon. My team had a tournament in Los Angeles so we flew to LA and arrived around 4:00 pm. We went into Long Beach's airport because my dad hates LAX. He says it's way too crowded and the last time we went there it took us over an hour to get from the main terminal to the rental car pavilion. Long Beach, by contrast, is nice and small and it cracks me up because you depart the plane right onto the tarmac, then walk straight to the baggage claim area, which is also outside. It doesn't get any quicker and easier than that. My dad rented a Camaro and it was really sweet. It was jet black and had a sunroof, leather interior, pumpin' stereo, and power everything. I couldn't wait until the other girls saw me in it. I knew they were going to die. Anyway, after we got our car we headed for our hotel in Irvine but we were hungry so we stopped along the way for dinner. We went to a restaurant on Newport Beach, right on the end of the pier, and we sat outside on the deck so Homer could be with us. I don't think dogs are actually allowed out there, even though it's outside, but the restaurant wasn't too busy and the waitress thought Homer was cute so she allowed it. We got sushi and it took forever for it to arrive but once it did, it was worth the wait. We got several different types and it was all good but the baked lobster was to die for. I've always liked sushi, especially nigiri and sashimi, but I've never had sushi that tasted quite like that before. I ate every piece and wanted more so we ordered another roll.

As we walked back to our car, we stopped at a booth and got some sunglasses since I forgot mine. Every trip, no matter how hard I try, I always forget something. I even got Homer a pair since they have doggy sunglasses in LA. LA is so cool, they have the craziest things. After that, we headed to our hotel, which was nice but nothing like the one we had stayed at in Las Vegas in the fall.

The next day, we had three games and they went relatively well. We won two of them and everyone played fine, and even the third game, the one we lost, was close. After that we went to Huntington Beach to goof around and have some fun and we got boogie boards, and we even put Homer on one. He went about ten feet before a wave hit him and blew him over, and everyone laughed as he doggy-paddled back to shore. After that, he was content to stay on the beach and watch us from there, and he chased away a seagull that landed on our blankets.

"Darn it," Kimi said. "I wish Homer had chased that seagull away a little faster."

"Why?" I asked.

She held up her blanket. Right in the middle of it was a big, white splotch.

Sucks to be her.

But the real drama happened later that night when we returned to our hotel. We were relaxing by the pool when Lea, Kimi, Kristin, and I decided we wanted some candy, so we walked across the street to the convenience store on the corner. It wasn't actually that far, and our hotel was still in sight, right across the road. Homer came with us on his leash. We got our goodies and were heading back to the hotel when two men stepped out of an alley and blocked our path down the sidewalk. One man was tall and thin, and the other was short and heavy, and they wore leather jackets that looked old and dirty. Neither man looked like he had shaved in a week, probably longer. The shorter man had a tattoo of a dragon on the side of his neck and a bullring in his nose. The taller man spoke first and the tone of his voice was really creepy. "What do we have here?"

The second man responded and he slurred his words as though he had been drinking. "Some young ladies out on the town looking for a good time, I'd guess."

We were completely caught off guard since none of us had seen them coming, and I instantly felt apprehensive and afraid. Lea took the initiative and addressed them. "We're just trying to get back to our hotel."

"Why do you want to do that?" the taller man asked. "A hotel is so boring on a night like tonight. Why don't you come and hang with us tonight? Leo and I will show you a good time."

At first, we didn't know what to say, so everyone was quiet. But finally Lea, who is by far the bravest one of us all, mustered an answer. "No thanks. We just want to go back to our hotel. Please step aside."

The taller man's eyes got big and it was obvious he had been offended. "I'm just trying to be friendly, little miss. I just want you to come with me for a while. I won't hurt you. Well, not too much."

He reached out and grabbed Lea by the wrist.

That was all it took. The minute he touched her, Homer tore from my grip, taking his leash with him as he went. He bared his teeth and growled louder than he's ever growled before. He hit the man squarely in the chest and blew him back onto the ground. The man was so surprised he didn't know what to do, and Homer grabbed him by an arm and shook him fiercely. The second man, the shorter one, came to his aid and kicked Homer in the side but Homer turned and fought him off, too, and he bit him on the leg, right above his knee. Before I could do anything, both men had decided they had had enough, and they turned and tried to run away, but it was already too late for them because a passing police officer had spotted the confrontation and cut them off with his squad car. Within seconds, the officer had pulled out his gun, handcuffed both of them, and loaded them into the back of his car.

"Are you ladies okay?"

We were still pretty shaken, especially Lea who was crying, but we were okay, and we were more concerned about Homer than ourselves. We wanted to make certain he was okay. Although the altercation had only lasted a few seconds, it had been extremely violent and Homer had been kicked in the side really hard. Luckily, however, he was okay and he was already calmed down and acting like normal, like nothing had ever happened.

The police officer smiled as he looked at him. "That's one heck of a dog you've got there. He's as brave as they get. I may have to recruit him for our K9 team."

With a smile, he escorted us back to our hotel and the minute our dads and the other girls saw us coming with a police escort, they got worried and came running. The officer explained everything. "I got there as soon as I could, but I'll be honest, I may not have gotten there in time if it wasn't for that dog. He saved the day. There's no doubt about it."

My team has always treated Homer well since he is our beloved mascot, but for the rest of the night he was treated like canine royalty. All thirteen girls gathered around him and started petting him at the same time, and then we took turns giving him hugs. He didn't appear to be injured but we put an icepack on his side just to be sure. And he loved every minute of it. He's always liked attention, especially from softball girls, so he was in doggy heaven. But the funniest thing of all was he acted like he hadn't done anything extraordinary at all. And to him he hadn't. After all, to him, we were his girls, and no one was going to hurt his girls when he was around.

June 6

I had a really bad nightmare last night. I dreamed the school year had ended and Logan had moved back to Texas and he had forgotten about me completely. The minute he stepped off of the plane in Texas, he forgot my name and he forgot about all of the wonderful things we had done during the past year. And then he got a new girlfriend, a high-maintenance cheerleader with red hair and a thick, southern accent. They went to one of his football games at his high school in Huckstin and she cheered and tossed her pompoms in the air as he scored a touchdown. After the touchdown, he ran off of the field, swept her up in his arms, and kissed her on the lips.

I awoke with a start and I was covered in sweat. I didn't sleep again that night.

June 7

I was sitting on the couch in the living room, watching television with my dad, when his cell phone rang. He glanced at the phone's screen and looked over at me with a puzzled expression on his face.

"That's funny. It's Chloe."

"Why's that funny?"

"She only sends me texts. I can't remember the last time she called me."

I nodded and it did make sense. Like most teenage girls, including me, Chloe preferred texting and she rarely made phone calls. Except to her boyfriend, Caleb, but that's because he doesn't like to text very much. Like a lot of teenage boys, he doesn't spell very well.

My dad shrugged and answered the phone. "Hey Chloe, what's up?" The expression on his face changed in a heartbeat. His smile disappeared and was replaced with a look of grave concern. "Chloe, listen to me. You need to calm down. I can't understand a word you're saying." He paused as he listened. "Are you okay? I don't care about your car. Are you okay?"

My mom was in the kitchen making dinner but she overheard the conversation and rushed into the room as fast as she could. She had a knife in one hand and a cucumber in the other. There was a look of complete panic on her face. From the small amount she had overheard, she knew something was wrong. So did I.

Luckily, the tone of my dad's voice changed quickly and grew much calmer. "Thank goodness. Tell me where you are. I'll come and get you. Okay, okay. No, it's okay. What? Yeah, I know where it is. I'll be there in a minute."

I could barely wait until he hung up to ask what had happened but my mom beat me to the punch. My dad answered as he was grabbing his keys and putting on his coat. "Chloe was in an accident. I need to go get her."

"Can I come?" I asked.

"Whatever," my dad said, but I could tell he was so preoccupied with his thoughts he barely heard my question.

My mom and Homer came with us. We arrived at the scene of the accident a few minutes later. It was on a small highway not too far from our house. My heart stopped the minute I saw Chloe's car. It was upside down in the ditch, on its top and hood, and it was completely demolished. The windshield was shattered and the entire side of the car was caved in. Two police cars and an ambulance were parked next to it, both with their lights on. A trio of paramedics was treating Chloe's injuries. She had a small cut on her left cheek and she looked totally distraught, but other than that she was okay.

My dad pushed his way through the paramedics and gave her a hug.

"Thank goodness you're okay. You had me pretty worried for a couple of minutes there, kiddo."

Tears ran from her eyes. "My car. It's destroyed. It's totally destroyed."

"It's okay. We can get you another one. I'll call the insurance company tomorrow morning and we'll take care of it. All that matters is you're okay."

She gave him another hug, then turned and gave my mom one, then me and Homer. Her face was red and her eyeliner was everywhere.

I couldn't help but ask what had happened.

"It was raining. I had my lights and my wipers on but I still couldn't see very well and I didn't see the exit until it was too late, but I tried to make it anyway. And the car flipped. Twice. I was so scared I thought I was going to die."

I didn't know what to say. I've never been in an accident like that so I couldn't really relate, but at the same time I could imagine how terrifying it must have been for her. I would have freaked out if I had been in a situation like that.

My dad was listening carefully and his face was as white as a ghost but I'll give him credit, he stayed completely calm. Since he had never wanted Chloe to have a car in the first place, I thought he was going to say something like, "I knew this was going to happen" or "I told you so" but he never did. Instead, he said, "Accidents happen. I'm just glad you're okay." Then he went and talked to the police officers and the paramedics and he made arrangements to get

Chloe's car towed to a wrecking yard, and then we went home. It was a sad night and Chloe was so upset she cried most of the night, but we were still thankful. At least she was okay.

June 10

Today was one of the best days ever. My school has two end-of-the-year dances. One is called senior prom and is for seniors and their dates. The other is called summer prom and is for everyone else. Senior prom is the more prestigious of the two, since you know what they say, it's all about the seniors, but summer prom is fun too and since I'm a freshman it was my first time to go so I was pretty excited. Lea and Kimi were fired up, too. Two players on the school's baseball team had asked them to go and both boys were really cute.

Like always, it took me a long time to get ready. I wanted everything to be perfect. Chloe had helped me pick out a dress a few days before and it was really cute, if I do say so myself. It was fancy, but not overly so, and it was solid black and it made me look really shapely, especially through the chest and hips. Of course my dad didn't like it because he felt it was 'way too tight' but I didn't care what he thought. I wore a pair of heels that weren't really that high but I had a beast of a time walking in them anyway, at least at first.

Chloe walked into the bathroom to help me with my final preparations. Normally, she would have been getting ready, too, but she and Caleb were going to senior prom the following night since Caleb was a senior. Her final assessment of me was a simple one. "I'm impressed."

Logan picked me up about twenty minutes later, wearing a black tuxedo, and he looked spectacular, even better than when he had worn a fancy suit on Valentine's Day. My parents took photos of us in the living room, we went to dinner, then to the dance. It was in the school's gymnasium and I must give the dance's organizers credit, they did a wonderful job. The gym was decorated with banners, lights, and streamers and it looked amazing. The music was loud, but not too bad, and there was a DJ. Lea and Kimi looked stunning, especially Lea. She's usually pretty tomboyish so to see her wearing an elegant dress with her hair down, it was special. We waited until a slow song began then headed onto the dance floor en masse. I wrapped my arms around Logan's neck as he placed his hands on my hips. I've always been so amazed. Logan has big hands so I like to tease him and call him an ogre, but even with big, ogre-sized hands, he is always so gentle when he touches me. We swayed slowly to the music, and I glanced around as we danced, and in the corner of the room I saw Hailey Wetmore standing quietly with her date, who was one of the backup players on the football team. She was looking right at me and she had an irritated and jealous look on her face. I don't think she's ever gotten over the fact Logan turned her down, nor the fact he chose to go steady with me instead of her. I smiled at her briefly, then leaned forward and kissed Logan on the lips.

"What was that for?" he asked.

"For being you," I said.

Just for curiosity's sake, I looked back over, toward where Hailey had been standing, but she was nowhere to be found.

June 15

Today was the last day of the school year, which is usually one of my favorite days of the year. Everyone is so excited, and I can finally start sleeping in every day, and there is no homework for three months. But despite all of that, I didn't like today at all. If I could have had it my way, I would have postponed it forever.

Today was the day Logan left.

He picked me up for a final date around 6:00 pm. He had to be at the airport at 8:00 pm for his flight to Dallas so it didn't give us much time, just over an hour, but it actually turned out to be more than enough. I had always pictured our final date as something grand and elegant and romantic, something I would remember and cherish forever, but it wasn't. I could tell from the start it wasn't meant to be. Logan wasn't himself. I could see it in his eyes. He's normally so upbeat and lively. But tonight he was lifeless and sad, a mere shell of himself. He tried his best to make the most of things but his smiles were forced and they were nothing more than an act, a final, desperate attempt to have some fun with me before his inevitable departure.

We went to dinner at a nice Mexican restaurant but we didn't say much. I guess there wasn't much to say and I guess we were just putting in our time, waiting for it all to be over. Twice I almost started to cry but somehow I managed to keep it together, even when he dropped me off at the door of my house. He had a note in his hand as he said goodbye.

"I knew I was going to have a tough time tonight and I didn't want to risk blowing my chance to tell you how I feel so I wrote it all down. But do me a favor and wait until after I leave before you read it. Okay?"

I nodded. I was in no mood to disagree with him about anything. "Have a safe flight. I miss you already."

"I miss you, too."

I gave him a kiss and he turned and left.

I rushed upstairs to my bedroom the minute he disappeared from view. I didn't even stop to say hi to Homer in the hallway like I normally do. I jumped on my bed and tore the envelope open as fast as I could. It read,

Angel,

I always thought you had the most appropriate name. To me, you've always been an angel. I knew you were special the minute I saw you in the bleachers that night at my game. I'm not certain when I will get to see you again but I promise I will never forget you. I will stay in touch and will hopefully get to come back to the Northwest soon. Or maybe you can come to Texas. I think you'd like it. Anyway, I

*love you. I've loved you from the moment
I saw you. And I always will.*

Logan

I sat there in complete shock as I read the letter. I was frozen in place, staring at the words on the paper, and it was at that point I first realized what love was. It was the most wonderful thing in the world but also the most awful. I was ecstatic to learn how Logan felt about me, but also so upset he was leaving and I might not get to see him again. I felt like my heart was going to tear itself in two.

A lone teardrop fell from my cheek and landed on the letter, right above Logan's name.

I sat there for what seemed like an eternity, completely paralyzed by my feelings, completely unable to move. Homer, who had jumped onto the bed next to me, could tell something was wrong and he nudged me with his nose but I didn't respond. Not knowing what else to do, he hopped from the bed and ran down the hall to get Chloe, who was brushing her teeth in the bathroom. He grabbed her by a pantleg and pulled her down the hall toward my room.

"Homer, what in the world has gotten into you? Angel, what's up with your—"

Her words trailed off as he pulled her around the corner and she saw me sitting on my bed, Logan's note still in my hands, my eyes filled with tears.

"Angel. What's wrong?"

I handed her the note. Her eyes got misty as she read it. All she said was, "Wow." And then she did the only thing she could to make me feel any better. She sat down and gave me a hug.

June 17

It hasn't been easy the past couple of days. Chloe is still recovering from her car accident and I'm still recovering from Logan moving back to Texas. I've kept pretty much to myself and I've spent a lot of time in my room with just Homer and Cinnamon. I sent a couple of texts to Logan and found out he made it back to Huckstin safely and it seems like everyone is really happy to have him back, especially his dad and brothers. They had a party for him and apparently everyone was there including several of his cousins he hadn't seen for years. It's hard for me to keep them all straight since I've never met them and they all have double names like Billy Joe, Tommy Lee, and Jim Bob. He said even his stepmother was happy to see him and she gave him a hug and apologized for the animosity between them the past couple of years. I told him I was happy for him and I wished him well.

I had softball practice today. It was my first practice since Logan left and it was actually pretty surprising. Well, not practice, it was extremely routine, but afterward. I had just gotten out of the shower and I was sitting on my bed, petting Homer and Cinnamon, when my dad knocked on my bedroom door. He had a cup of hot chocolate in one hand and a saucer with a blueberry muffin in the other.

"Can I come in?"

"Sure."

"I thought you might like a snack. I know I worked you guys pretty hard at practice today so you must be hungry."

"A little." Actually, I wasn't, and I haven't had much of an appetite since Logan left, but since my dad went to the trouble of bringing it to me I thought I'd be polite and take it. And it was pretty good, especially the hot chocolate. My dad isn't much of a chef but he is pretty good when it comes to using a microwave.

He sat down on the edge of my bed. I could tell he wanted to say something but he wasn't exactly sure how to say it. "I wanted to ask you something. I noticed at practice today you seemed pretty listless. Your effort was good, you definitely were trying, there's no disputing that, but you just weren't your normal self. Your throws didn't have much zip on them and you didn't have any spring in your step. Your sprint times were your worst in years."

I sighed. I knew what was coming next. I was in trouble.

"You're heartbroken, aren't you?"

My eyes got big. I couldn't believe what I had just heard. My dad, who was arguably the most insensitive person on the planet, had figured out what was wrong with me? I was in complete shock. Who was this strange doppelgänger and what had he done with my real dad?

"You haven't been the same since Logan left. I can see it. It doesn't take a rocket scientist to figure it out. And I want you to know it's okay. I've been there myself."

"What? What do you mean?"

"I'll show you."

He got up, went down the hall, and climbed into the attic. We have one of those attics you can enter through a small opening in the ceiling in the hallway. It has a door that covers the opening and an extendable ladder that descends from the door when you open it. Technically, Chloe and I aren't allowed to go up there since my dad says it's dangerous but we used to sneak up there all of the time when my parents weren't around. We keep all kinds of stuff up there like our fake Christmas tree and other holiday and yard decorations. There are some dead electronics up there too since for some unkown reason my dad didn't want to get rid of them. Anyway, he disappeared for at least ten minutes and I could hear him digging through things, clearly looking for something in particular, and then I heard him grimace.

"What happened?"

"I stepped in a cobweb."

I cringed. I hated cobwebs. Better him than me.

A few minutes later, he came back down with something in his hand. It was an old shoebox and it was tattered and worn and it looked like it was at least a hundred years old, maybe older. He sat down next to me on the bed and opened it, revealing its contents, which were a bunch of crinkled photos.

"What's this?"

"Some stuff I should have thrown out years ago but didn't. Sometimes memories are hard to shake, I guess. Anyway, this is what I wanted to show you."

He dug through the shoebox and pulled out an old photo. It was faded and it looked like it had been taken a long time ago but it was still nice and it was of an attractive girl, approximately eighteen, who had long, brown hair and sparkling eyes.

"This is Jennifer Snow. She was my girlfriend in high school."

"You had a girlfriend before mom?"

"Of course I had a girlfriend before your mom. Several. I mean, well, a few. Anyway, Jennifer and I were a couple from the beginning of our junior year until we graduated."

I was surprised. I never knew much about my dad's life before my birth. He never really talked about it much, other than football, and I guess it was just kind of hard for me to picture that he was more than just my dad. He was a real person and he had actually been a teenager once, just like me, and he had gone to high school and had had a girlfriend.

"What was she like?"

"Wonderful, in every way. She was the prettiest, sweetest girl I'd ever met. But don't tell your mom I said that or there will be repercussions. Anyway, she was smart, and kind, and we got along so well. She loved history just like I do. Some days we would just sit around and talk about how cool it would be to have a time machine and travel back to earlier times, back in China, or Rome, or the wild, wild west, or whenever. It was really nice."

Sitting around talking about the ancient past wasn't my cup of tea, but if that's what turned my dad on, so be it.

"She was the first girl I ever loved. I went and saw her every chance I got."

"What happened to her?"

"Same thing that happens to most high school couples. Once we graduated, she went to a college back east and I stayed here and went to Washington. Like all couples, we exchanged letters for a while but eventually she met someone new, and eventually I met someone new, and we moved on. But that isn't my point. What I wanted to tell you was those first few weeks, after she moved back east, that was the hardest time of my life. I was so lonely I thought I was going to die. I didn't see how I could go on without her."

"What did you do?"

"Not much, really. There wasn't much I could do. I just gave it some time and slowly I started to heal. And that's what you need to do now. Don't rush things and don't try to recover too quickly. Just be patient and give yourself some time. And if you need a small break from softball, that's okay, too. I understand. It'll suck for me since I won't have my star shortstop but that's the way it goes sometimes."

I was in complete shock. My dad had never been so understanding in his entire life, at least not with me, and he had never let me skip a practice before, except the one time a few years back when I had a fever and my temperature was 102°.

"Thanks, but I don't understand. Why didn't you show me this photo before?"

"This was a tough time for me. The toughest time in my life. Sometimes I try to forget it completely. Even now, after all these years, when I think about it, it still hurts."

I was completely amazed. This was a side of my dad I had never seen before.

Then something caught my eye. The shoebox contained other stuff including a bunch of newspaper clippings. "What's this?"

"Some articles from when I played ball."

I grabbed one of the articles and read it. Its headline said, "MONROE BEATS LAKE STEVENS 21-6." Below the headline was a photo of my dad in a football uniform, celebrating in the end zone with his teammates.

"That was a fun game. It was my junior year. I scored two touchdowns, including the game winner."

I grabbed another article. This one said, "WILLIAMS LEADS MONROE TO VICTORY." Below it was another photo of my dad, again in the end zone, with a smile on his face.

I was impressed. I had always known my dad played football in high school but I never knew he was so good.

"But they're not all pleasant," my dad said. "Look at this one."

He handed me an article with another photo. In this one, he was lying on the ground on his back, near the sideline, with a glazed look in his eyes. The trainers were treating him. The headline read, "WILLIAMS INJURED IN LOSS TO EDMONDS."

"What happened?"

"I was stupid. We ran a sweep right and I already had the first down, so I could have stepped out of bounds and avoided any contact whatsoever, but I got cocky and tried to cut back for a few more yards. The linebacker put his head down and hit me helmet-to-helmet. Nowadays that would be a penalty, but not back then. He hit me so hard it knocked me completely out of bounds and onto the ground. I was so stunned when I finally started to recover, I realized everyone in the stands was completely quiet and the cheerleaders were down on one knee, so I knew someone was injured. I looked around to see who it was and finally realized everyone was looking at me."

"Did they take you out of the game?"

"No. Back in those days, they didn't take you out just because you got a concussion. They didn't know much about concussions back then, how dangerous they can be. They just gave me a small break, had me sniff some smelling salts, then sent me back out. But I wasn't the same after that and I didn't play well. We got killed."

He looked kind of somber for a minute but his mood changed when he saw another article. "Here's a funny one." It had a photo of him catching a pass with a defender right behind him. "In this game, a guy hit me in the stomach, and he hit me so hard I walked over to the sideline and threw up right there on the spot. I didn't even have time to take my helmet off so the vomit went right through my facemask."

"Gross."

"Totally. But that wasn't the most amazing part. When I got done puking, I looked up and my coach was standing over me with a hand on my shoulder, and do you know what he said?"

"What?"

"He said, 'Are you done yet?' And when I said I was, he said, 'Good. Get back on the field. Sweep left on three.' Not knowing what else to do, I headed out and finished the game, and I actually did pretty well. I scored two touchdowns."

I laughed. "That reminds me of the time a few years back at Chloe's game, I think they were playing the Wolverines. Do you remember how she said she had an upset stomach but her coach made her play anyway and she hit a single, but as soon as she got to first base she kept running and went straight off the field and got sick behind the Wolverines' dugout?"

My dad laughed. "That was pretty funny. I've never seen anyone run straight off of the field before. She didn't even call a timeout. Even Blue thought it was hilarious. But poor Chloe. She was miserable after that."

He wasn't kidding. She got the flu and was sick for over a week.

We looked through the articles for a couple more minutes. I couldn't believe how many there were. And then I noticed something interesting.

"Your uniforms. They were black. And your helmets, too. Now we wear orange."

"They must have changed them after I graduated. And thank goodness it happened after I graduated. There's no way I'd be caught dead wearing those orange uniforms you kids wear nowadays."

I laughed. My dad was so predictable and so traditional. Of course he'd prefer old-school black to neon orange.

"Did you notice something else about my uniform? Look at my number."

I looked at one of the photos and saw my dad's jersey number. He wore number 24. The same number as Logan.

"Apparently," he said, "it's a Monroe tradition. The great running backs always wear number 24."

I didn't really know what to say. Thinking of Logan made me sad again but I had to admit, overall, I felt a little better. I couldn't believe it but my dad had actually cheered me up at least for a little while.

He stood up. "I should be going but feel free to keep the articles if you'd like."

I nodded. "I'd like to read a few more if it's okay."

"Of course. Hang in there, kid. Things will be okay."

With a smile, he turned and left.

July 14

Today was the first day of Washington's annual championship tournament. It's a huge event that lasts an entire week and features the best teams from all over the state. It's really fun but extremely stressful. It's a single elimination tournament so you get to keep playing until you lose a game. Once you lose, you're out of the tournament and your season is over.

Our first game was against a team from Spokane called the Tomahawks. They wore uniforms that caught my attention immediately because they had Native American symbols and imagery which I didn't think was allowed anymore. Anyway, Laura pitched a gem of a game and the final score was 2-1. Olivia won it for us with a double in the fifth inning that scored Haley from third base and Kimi from first. I got two singles and a double.

Our second game was against a team from Puyallup called the Pressure. Once again, we played well and we won 6-4. I didn't get any hits but I made several nice plays in the field. One of them was a running backhanded catch that saved at least one run, maybe two. Everyone patted me on the back and Homer gave me an affectionate lick as I returned to the dugout.

But the best game by far was the day's finale. It was against a team called the Avalanche. I had never heard of them before and I had no idea where they were from but boy were they good. They jumped to a quick lead and held on from there. The score was 2-0 going into the final inning and things were looking really bleak for us. The end of our season was only two outs away when, thankfully, we made a breakthrough. Casey and Kimi got singles, Lea walked to load the bases, then Kristin hit a bases-clearing triple to win it for us. We swarmed her at third base and tackled her right there on the spot and it was one of the greatest pig piles ever. Everyone joined in, including Homer, and at one point he got flipped onto his back and buried beneath a pile of bodies, but he didn't care because to him it was nothing but fun and games.

July 19

Today was the penultimate day of the championship tournament and everyone was excited. Our game was against a team called the Everett Extreme and we knew if we won we'd be in the finals the next day, and as such we couldn't wait. The game went well from the start. Hannah was our starting pitcher and she didn't give up a single hit until the fifth inning. In the meantime, our bats were fruitful and we jumped to a lead when Lea and Laura got back-to-back singles and I brought them in with a double. In no time, we were up 2-0. Everyone was in a good mood and was completely fired up. Even Blue was in a good mood, and it was the same Blue who umpires a lot of our games, the same one who likes Homer so much. Anyway, we were leading 7-0 in the final inning and there was only one out to go. Victory was so close I could taste it. The state's championship game, the biggest game of the year by far, was only one out away.

But then disaster struck. The one thing I never imagined possible, the nightmare of nightmares. I was standing at my position at short and the batter was a girl named Mandy McCormick. Mandy is a good hitter but nothing special so I knew we had a decent chance to get her out and end the game, but I was taking nothing for granted and was manning my position at short attentively. Mandy hit a pitch over the backstop and into the adjacent parking lot and like always, Homer darted after it. He loved foul balls. In the meantime, as he was retrieving it, the game continued since Blue had another ball. The next pitch was a fastball and Mandy missed it badly.

I could barely contain my excitement.

Only one strike to go, I thought. *One more strike and we're in the championship game.*

But then I heard a loud screech from the parking lot, like someone had slammed on the brakes and slid their tires, and it was followed by a dull thud and a painful yelp. When I looked over to see what had happened, I saw a large truck and a man climbing out of the driver's seat with a frantic, frightened look on his face. And when I looked in front of the truck, I saw Homer, lying on the pavement, with a softball on the ground next to him.

And he wasn't moving.

My heart stopped. I didn't even wait for Blue to call a timeout. I threw my mitt down and ran as fast as I could. And I wasn't the only one. Every girl on my team, even the girls in the dugout, ran for the parking lot with me. When we got there, Homer was finally moving but barely. The truck had hit him really hard. Tears streamed down my cheeks as I saw him lying there. He was trying to get up but he couldn't. He was so disoriented he could barely tell one direction from another. Finally, he gave up and fell onto his side.

The driver was frantic. "I'm sorry. I didn't see him until it was too late. I tried to stop."

My dad took over. He, too, had rushed to the parking lot with us. "We need to get him to a vet."

As if on cue, a car raced up. Blue was driving. "Come with me. I know the closest animal hospital."

"What about the game? It's not over."

"Screw the game. That dog helped me all year. Now it's my turn to help him."

My dad scooped Homer up and we climbed in the car and raced down the street. Blue was not obeying the speed limit but I wasn't going to complain. Luckily, the animal hospital wasn't far and it only took us five minutes to get there, maybe less. We ran inside and the veterinarian was waiting for us upon arrival since my dad had called and told him we were coming. He took Homer into the back and immediately started an examination and treatment. In the meantime, I stayed in the waiting room with Blue, my dad, and several of the other girls, who had arrived at the animal hospital shortly after we had.

And then I lost it. Completely. I was already crying, even before we got to the animal hospital, but now I was a complete wreck. It was a complete, uncontrollable flood of emotion. In my mind, I had already lost Logan, possibly forever, and I couldn't bear the thought of losing Homer, too. I collapsed in a chair and cried my eyes out. My dad, Blue, and the other girls rushed over to try to comfort me.

"Hang in there, young lady," Blue said. "Everything's going to be okay. Homer's a tough dog. He'll pull through."

Thankfully, he was right. The vet came out about twenty minutes later, which seemed like an eternity to me, and said Homer had three broken ribs and a fractured front leg, but ultimately he was going to be okay. I've never felt so relieved in my entire life.

"But I need to keep monitoring him just to be safe. I need to make certain there's no internal bleeding or other damage. So I'm going to keep him for observation here at the hospital overnight."

I objected. "He's never been away from me for a night. I can't leave him. I'll stay here with him."

The vet smiled but would not grant my request. "I can't allow that. It's against the hospital's policy. But don't worry. We'll take good care of him and you can come get him tomorrow afternoon. I should know by then whether he's okay or not."

"Tomorrow afternoon? We have our game first thing in the morning. He's our mascot and he's never missed a game before. We can't play without him."

"I'm sorry. He's just not going to be ready by then. You girls will have to make do without him."

I didn't know what to say and I was overwhelmed with conflicting emotions. I was relieved because I knew Homer was going to be okay, I was heartbroken because he couldn't come home with me, and I was disappointed because he had to miss the championship game.

My dad tried to help me feel a little better. "I know you're upset but remember the big picture. He'll be back with us tomorrow night and that's all that matters, right? He's okay."

I didn't want to admit it but he was right. Things could have been worse. Homer could have died.

So we went back to the field where everyone, including our fans and the other team, was still waiting. They were relieved to hear Homer was going to be okay but completely bummed when they learned he couldn't come to the championship game the next day.

But then I remembered something. Technically, we weren't in the championship game yet. We still had one strike to go. Were they going to make us go back onto the field to finish the game? After all that had happened, and after all I had gone through, I didn't feel like playing any more.

Luckily, I didn't have to. Blue met with the coaches to discuss things and the Extreme's coach put an end to everything immediately.

"I don't think it's fair to make the girls come out and play again just for one batter. They've been through so much already, losing their mascot. As such, we concede, and we wish you well in tomorrow's game."

My dad shook his hand. "I can't thank you enough. This means a lot to us."

"You're a great team. You deserve to be in the championship game. And I hope Homer gets better soon. He may not be our mascot but we like him anyway."

How nice, I thought. Over the years, I had seen a lot of coaches and many of them were complete idiots. All they cared about was their own team and they would do anything to win. But not this guy. Clearly all he cared about was doing the right thing. I wish there were more coaches like him.

We packed up our stuff and went home. It wasn't that far of a drive but it seemed like it took forever. All I could think about was Homer. I called Logan in Texas and told him what had happened and he tried to make me feel better and it helped a little but not too much. I moped around the house for most of the night and when I finally went to bed, I couldn't get to sleep. I was so used to having Homer on the bed next to me I couldn't get comfortable without him being there. Even grumpy old Cinnamon seemed affected. He looked around the room, as if he knew something was amiss, then shot a questioning glance at me, as if to say, "Where is he?"

He'll be back soon, I thought.

And as far as I was concerned, it couldn't be soon enough.

July 20

The championship game did not start well. It was against my old team, the Eastside Angels, and my archrival, Ashley Martinez. We knew it was going to be a tough game to win but Ashley and the Angels weren't the problem.

The problem was us. Without Homer, we weren't ourselves, not at all. We were completely flat, completely uninspired. We were so accustomed to having him there, leading us during our warm-up drills and barking happily whenever we made a great play, we just didn't know what to do without him. The entire dugout was somber. There were a few cheers here and there but nothing like normal.

We got off to a bad start. Everyone struggled, including Laura, who was pitching. She couldn't get motivated and she couldn't throw strikes, at least not consistently. She walked the first two batters, then gave up a single to load the bases.

There was a look of urgency and grave concern on my dad's face. "She's got to hit her spots or we're gonna be in trouble. Big trouble."

And we were. Much to my chagrin, she didn't hit her spots and instead left a pitch over the middle of the plate. The Angels' shortstop, Brooke Conrad, lined it down the first base foul line for a double. Two runs scored on the play.

Just like that, we were losing 2-0.

The second inning didn't get any better. Laura continued to struggle and the Angels scored two more runs.

My dad shook his head. "I've got no choice. I've got to pull her."

So Laura and Hannah came into the dugout and my dad went out to talk to Blue, and like always we girls waited to see if the twins were going to do their normal routine and switch jerseys so Laura could keep pitching. But unlike normal, Laura didn't want to.

"I'm done. I can't focus."

But then Hannah responded, "I don't want to pitch, either."

It was a disaster. We only had two pitchers and neither of them wanted to pitch.

Hannah didn't have a choice since my dad had already reported the switch to Blue, so she took over, somewhat begrudgingly, and she didn't do any better than Laura. She gave up two runs and by the end of the third inning we were losing 6-0.

We didn't help any with our bats. We were terrible. We didn't get any hits at all and I struck out twice. Ashley wasn't throwing that well and I think she was actually having some control issues but it just didn't matter. Against us, she could have been the worst pitcher in the world and she would have done fine.

Chloe had come to watch and, from the bleachers, she saw what was happening. She came into the dugout and tried to fire us up but it didn't do much good. And unfortunately she couldn't help us by pitching since this was a 16u tournament so she was too old to play.

We had to win this one on our own. Without Chloe and without Homer.

But it wasn't going to happen. We all knew it. We were just putting in our time, trying to get it over with as quickly and as painlessly as possible.

But then something unexpected happened. From the parking lot, I heard a bark. I looked over and my eyes got big as I saw the veterinarian from the animal hospital, climbing out of a small, white van, and he had Homer in his arms. Homer had a splint on his front leg and his body was wrapped in a bandage of some sort, but other than that he looked like he was okay and he looked really hyper. He was squirming around in the vet's arms and he howled happily when he saw us in the distance.

Lea was the first one to say anything. "It's Homer! He's here."

I met the vet at the edge of the field. "What happened? I thought you said he couldn't come."

"I had no choice. He went crazy. He wouldn't stop barking all morning. It was like he knew you had a game."

"Of course he knew. He always knows when we have games. I'm not sure how but he does."

It was true. On game days, Homer was always the first one up. Sometimes at 3:00 am, which never made me happy.

We swarmed him. Every girl on the team gave him a hug, a kiss, and a pat on the head, and he gave us licks in return.

That was all it took. When we returned to the field, we were a completely different team. It was like someone had gotten rid of us and replaced us with good players. And it was all because we were excited and motivated again.

Chloe rallied us from the dugout. "Win this one for Homer."

"For Homer!" we shouted.

We poured it on. All of a sudden, Hannah could pitch again, and she could pitch well. She threw nothing but strikes, as hard as she could, and the Angels' batters were completely overwhelmed. Even Brooke, who is one of the best batters I've ever seen, was no match for her. In the meantime, our bats came alive. Lea and Kimi hit singles, Haley got a triple, and I got a double. Boy it felt good to finally get a hit off of Ashley. I heard her grimace as I slid into second base.

In no time, we were back in it. We had gotten three runs and we were determined to get more. When the final inning began, we wasted no time loading the bases.

And here's the best part. Guess who was the next batter? You guessed correctly. As I stepped into the batter's box I turned and looked at Ashley with a look of pure determination in my eyes. I was a completely different batter than I had been at the start of the game. At the start, I had been timid and weak, a pitiful excuse for a player. But now I was confident and strong. Homer was there, and with him there, I was ready to take on the world.

And then I remembered what Logan had told me right before I had gone on my trip to Vegas in the fall. He had wanted me to hit a home run for him but I wasn't sure I could do it.

"Have faith in yourself," he had said. "I know you can do it."

In Vegas, I had. I had hit a home run. And in the championship game, facing my greatest rival, with the bases loaded, I did it again. Ashley's first pitch was a wicked fastball, one of her best of the day. I knew I shouldn't swing at it since it was a little low but I went after it anyway, with everything I had, and I hit it so hard it flew a mile. It didn't start to descend until long after it had cleared the outfield fence.

July 25

Today was my team's 'end of the season' party. Like every end of the season party, it was a little sad since some of the girls would be moving on to other teams next year, but overall it was a good time and I had fun. It was at Lea's house and the weather was nice so we got to wander back and forth, inside and out. Some people played horseshoes in the back yard while others mingled in the kitchen or on the patio. There was a lot of food and I stuffed myself. After eating, we watched a funny video my dad had made that was basically a slideshow of photos he had rounded up over the course of the season. It brought back some fond memories and made me realize how quickly time had gone by. One of the photos really caught my eye. It was a shot of me batting and sitting in the bleachers behind me was Logan.

After the video, my dad gave the traditional head coach end of the season speech and he actually did pretty well considering it was the first time he had given a head coach end of the season speech. What he said was pretty generic and it was the same stuff you hear every year, and I think he even ripped off a few jokes from one of my previous coaches, but even so it was amusing. And then he handed out the awards and that was great. Laura won the most valuable pitcher award, Kristin won the comeback player of the year award, Olivia won the most improved award, Lea won the gold glove award for the best defensive player, and I won the silver slugger award for the best hitter. I got a trophy that was shaped like a bat and was covered in sparkling, black chrome.

But the best award of all, the most prestigious by far, was the final one presented by my dad and it was the one Homer won. It was the team's MVP award.

Most Valuable Pooch.

It was actually just a round cookie with yellow icing, but Homer loved it and everyone cheered as he gobbled it up.

Glossary of Softball Terms

At-bat: A player's turn to bat while her team is on offense. Players take turns batting. In a typical seven inning game, a player will usually get three or four at-bats.

Batting Order: The order in which batters take turns hitting during a game. The batting order is usually chosen by the team's coach or its manager at the beginning of the game. The batter who bats first is called the 'leadoff hitter,' and the fourth batter is called the 'cleanup hitter.' Many players see it as a promotion to be moved up in the order (closer to the leadoff batter), since they will get more at-bats per game, and they see it as a demotion to be moved down in the order.

Ball: A pitch that travels outside of the strike zone that the hitter does not swing at. If a pitcher throws four balls to a batter, before she gets three strikes, it results in a walk.

Blue: An informal term used to refer to the umpires. It originates from the traditional color of their uniforms.

Bunt: A soft hit produced by holding the bat in a stationary position over home plate. Bunts are often used strategically to advance a base runner to the next base. There are several different types of bunts, including 'sacrifice bunts' and 'push bunts.' During a sacrifice bunt, the batter intentionally tries to bunt the ball in a way so the defensive players will throw her out at first, thus allowing a base runner to advance safely to the next base. During a push bunt, a batter tries to reach first base safely by pushing the ball between the defenders just out of their reach.

Change-up: A pitch that is thrown to a batter much slower than a pitcher's other pitches. It is also called a 'change.'

Count: The term used to describe a batter's balls and strikes during her at-bat. The number of balls is listed first, followed by the number of strikes. If blue says, "The count is two and one," he's telling everyone the batter has two balls and one strike.

Curveball: A pitch that curves as it heads toward home plate.

Double play: A play in which the defense records two outs. If the same player makes both outs, with no help from any other player, it is called an 'unassisted double play.'

Error: A ruling charged to a defensive player if she makes a mistake that should have resulted in an out.

Fair ball: A ball that, when hit, lands between the two foul lines and stays in bounds past first or third base. A home run is considered a fair ball.

Fastball: A type of pitch thrown to a batter. It is usually extremely fast (thus, the name).

Fastpitch: Fastpitch is a type of softball where the pitcher is allowed to pitch the ball as hard and as fast as she wants. In slowpitch softball, the pitcher is not allowed to throw the ball hard.

Fielders: The players who are playing defense and trying to get the batters and runners out.

Fly ball: A ball that is hit high into the air and is usually caught by the defenders.

Fly out: A ball that is caught by one of the defensive players before it touches the ground. The batter is out as soon as the ball is caught.

Force out: After a batter hits the ball, she must advance to first base. The defensive players can get her out by throwing the ball to first base before she reaches it. Additionally, other base runners must advance to the next base if they are forced by a base runner behind them.

Foul ball: A ball hit outside of the two foul lines. It results in a strike. If a batter already has two strikes when she hits a foul ball, the count remains the same and the at-bat continues, because a foul cannot result in a strikeout. A 'foul tip' is a type of foul ball that is hit directly behind the batter.

Ground ball: A ball hit on the ground in the infield.

Ground-rule double: A hit that lands in fair territory and bounces over the outfield fence. The batter is awarded second base, and all of the runners who were on base at the time advance two bases.

Hit: A batted ball that allows the batter to safely reach base. There are several types of hits. A single is a hit that allows a batter to advance to first base. A double is a hit that allows the batter to advance to second. A triple is a hit that allows a batter to advance to third base, and a home run is a hit that allows the batter to advance all the way to home plate.

Hit and run: A play where the base runner advances to the next base as soon as the pitcher releases the ball. Usually, the batter attempts to hit the ball regardless of whether it is a ball or a strike.

Home run: A hit that allows the batter to reach home plate safely. There are several types of home runs. An out-of-the-park home run is a hit that flies over the outfield fence between the two foul poles. The batter and any runners that are on base at the time are awarded home plate and each of them scores a run. An inside-the-park home run is a hit that does not fly over the outfield fence, but the batter reaches home plate anyway. A solo home run is a home run that occurs when there are no base runners on base, and a grand slam is a home run that occurs when there is a base runner on first, second, and third bases. In Seattle, a grand slam is called a 'Grand Salami' — a term coined by the legendary sportscaster Dave Niehaus.

Inning: The individual segments of a game. Each game has seven innings. Each team gets to bat once during each inning, and it gets to continue batting, and scoring runs, until the other team makes three outs. The visiting team bats first, in what is called the 'top' of the inning, and the home team bats second, in the 'bottom' of the inning.

Line drive: A ball that is hit very hard and with a trajectory almost parallel to the ground. Players are taught to hit line drives, because it is often very difficult for the defensive players to catch them.

No-hitter: A game in which the pitcher does not allow the opposing team to get any hits. No-hitters are extremely rare, and they are seldom done by any player at any level.

Out: The defense must create three 'outs' before an inning is over.

Power hitter: A batter who is known for hitting the ball extremely hard.

Riseball: A type of pitch that starts low, like a fastball, but rises dramatically as it heads toward home plate. Many batters (including Fastpitch Fever's star, Rachel Adams) are fooled by riseballs and they swing too low and miss them.

Robbed: A term used by players to describe a play in which they lose a hit, usually because a defensive player makes an outstanding play. In Fastpitch Fever, Rachel Adams was robbed of a hit in the state's championship game when the opposing center fielder dove and caught the ball. The girl who inspired *Fastpitch Fever*, Molly McCall, was robbed on a daily basis.

Run: A run is scored when a base runner safely reaches home plate.

Sacrifice: A play where a batter intentionally hits the ball into an out situation so she can advance or score a runner.

Safe: A ruling made by blue when a base runner safely reaches a base.

Screwball: A pitch that curves toward the side of the plate from which it was thrown.

Slapper: A left-handed batter known primarily for using her speed to get to first base.

Stolen base: A play in which a runner advances safely to the next base as soon as the pitcher releases the pitch.

Strike: A pitch that a batter swings at and misses, hits foul, or fails to swing at that crosses the strike zone. A batter is out after receiving three strikes.

Strike out: A play when a batter accumulates three strikes, at which point her at-bat ends and she is out.

Strike zone: The area above home plate between a batter's knees and armpits.

Tag out: A play in which a fielder with the ball tags a base runner who is not standing on a base.

Tag up: A base runner cannot leave a base until a batted ball hits the ground. If she does, and if the ball is caught, she must return to her base. If she waits until the ball is caught, then leaves the base, the play is called a 'tag up' and she is allowed to go.

The Cycle: A term used by players to describe the 'holy grail' of softball. A player hits for the cycle when she hits a single, double, triple, and home run in the same game. It is extremely hard to do and rarely done by any player at any level. The girl who inspired *Fastpitch Fever*, Molly McCall, hit for a 'super cycle' during one of her Little League games: she hit a single, double, triple, home run, and she was intentionally walked by the opposing pitcher.

Triple play: A play in which the defense records three outs. If the same player makes all three outs, with no help from any other players, it is called an 'unassisted triple play.' Triple plays are extremely rare.

Walk: Four balls from a pitcher results in the batter receiving a 'walk,' and the batter automatically advances to first base. A walk is also referred to as a 'base on balls.' An 'intentional walk' is a type of walk where the pitcher intentionally throws four balls, and she does not even try to get the batter out. Intentional walks are done to avoid pitching to really good batters in key situations.

About the Author

Jody Studdard is the author of several children's novels, including *A Different Diamond, Fastpitch Fever, Escape from Dinosaur Planet,* and *The Sheriff of Sundown City.* He is a graduate of Monroe High School (1989), the University of Washington (1993), and California Western School of Law (1995). In addition to writing, he is a practicing attorney with an office in Everett, Washington. He is a fan of the Seahawks, Storm, Sounders FC, and Kraken.

E-mail Jody at:

jodystuddard@gmail.com

SOFTBALL STAR
books by
Jody Studdard

A Different Diamond
Fastpitch Fever
Dog in the Dugout
Missfits Fastpitch
Silence in Center

Coming Soon!

Fastpitch U

KIANA CRUISE
books by
Jody Studdard

Apocalypse
Multiplicity

Made in United States
Orlando, FL
19 December 2021

12120617R10117